Bits of Broken Glass

MARTHA REYNOLDS

DEDICATION

for Kellies and Joes everywhere

MARTHA REYNOLDS

ACKNOWLEDGMENTS

My twenty-fifth high school reunion was one of the most enjoyable times I've ever had. The characters in this book are purely fictional, and not based on anyone I knew in school.

Thank you to my dear friend Lynne Marran Radiches, who listened for hours to my storytelling, when this novel was just a bunch of ideas and thoughts.

Thank you to my friend Gerri Fox, who was instrumental in helping me to understand the complexities of living with a diagnosis of breast cancer. The Susan G. Komen Breast Cancer Foundation and the Mayo Clinic also provided a wealth of online information.

To Francine LaSala – author, editor, and friend – thank you for your brilliant insight into capsulizing the essence of this story.

Finally, to my husband Jim, my love, my life. I'm the lucky one.

1

June 24 – 159 days to go

Monday mornings in the summer were the worst. Even before the clock radio next to her bed flipped on with strains of Vivaldi or Bach (composers more suited to morning classical radio than Tchaikovsky or Wagner, she supposed), the sun stared her down and Kellie surrendered. She folded back the light blanket and soft cotton sheet and stretched her arms and legs. Her toes pointed out like a ballerina's and her fingers splayed as she touched the wall behind her head. She tried to do a few sit-ups in bed, but gave up after three and swung her legs over the side. She squinted back at the sun and tucked her feet into scuff slippers. Just another day.

It used to be that Kellie didn't see the morning sun until she was out of her condo and on her way to work, but then the high-rise building across the street was torn down. She'd heard there would be a new, twenty-story office tower going up, but the developer ran out of money and now there was just a big square of rubble where a tall concrete rectangle once stood. It was an ugly block anyway, a giant gray edifice with no aesthetic charm. At least my building has character, Kellie thought. She lived on the fifth floor, the top floor of what used to be the Benoni Wilbur Stark Building. Kirby, who stood guard in the lobby most evenings, told her it used to be a brokerage house, back in the fifties and sixties, and the top floor, where she lived now, held executive suites and a large conference room. Her windows ran from floor to ceiling, about twelve feet, and when she moved in four months ago, she had to wait nearly three weeks for custom blinds to be made and installed. Kellie's condo took up half of the fifth floor, and faced east and south. Her neighbors, the Conways, had the north and west sides. Kellie thinks hers is better.

She padded to the kitchen and prepared the Keurig. It was a sensible purchase, she told herself last month as she handed over a hundred bucks for a coffeemaker. She picked up the remote and turned on the morning news, just in time to watch Marco segue from a brutal stabbing outside the city to a sunny forecast throughout the state. It was just before six and the day looked promising. Well, at least the weather did.

"Breaking news, this just coming in. A shooting in the capital city early this morning has resulted in two fatalities. All we know from the police at this time is that a man apparently shot and killed his live-in girlfriend, then turned the gun on himself. We'll continue to update you with any new information we receive."

Kellie used the remote to silence the television. She'd know all the details soon enough, and would probably be asked to put together some background story on the unfortunate couple. She finished her coffee, washed the mug in the sink, and turned it upside down to air dry on a rack.

She packed her tote the same way every morning: work shoes wrapped in a plastic grocery bag at the bottom; apple, yogurt, clean spoon, granola bar tucked into an insulated lunch bag; and whatever work she'd brought home the previous evening slid into the front flap. Her little makeup bag went on top once she was done with the morning application. She tapped the side pocket that held her pepper spray.

A quick shower and blow-dry and she opened the closet door to find the outfit she'd chosen the night before, hanging on the inside door. She'd learned in college to prepare her clothes in advance, and it had served her well for the past twenty years. As she lifted the hanger, Kellie glanced at the rows of shirts, skirts, jackets, dresses, and slacks, and a memory bubbled up, but only for an instant. There wasn't time to think back. And it did no good, anyway.

By ten o'clock, Kellie was twenty minutes into a boring conference call. Elizabeth had a meeting that she deemed more important, so she had Kellie sit in on the call. As she listened to nine other producers from around the region talk about the latest trends in reporting, her mind veered away from the discussion and she stared out her office window at the sharp blue day. The river that edged around the office building looked clean, with sun sparkles dancing along a lazy current. Two gray squirrels ran tandem through the park and a brown delivery truck rolled over the bridge. From her position on the fourth floor, Kellie had a view of the little park that sat next to the river: a small green rectangle situated between the asphalt and brick. Two skinny boys with skateboards and droopy pants slouched past rows of bright pink flowers.

Her computer pinged with the announcement of a new email message. The monotonous voice of the speaker on the call had lulled her into a dreamlike complacency and she was startled by the interruption. She touched a button on her phone to mute the speaker, and stretched her arms over her head, curling her neck to the right, then to the left, feeling the pull of muscles. As she read the message, Kellie sensed the same uneasiness in her stomach like that time she had to recite a poem in front of her fifth-grade class.

To: Kellie Campbell
From: Suzanne Fitch
Date: June 24, 2013
Re: You Won't Believe This

Got an email from Cherry Weiss this morning – remember her? 25-year HS reunion this November! First reunion we've ever had!! Guess she stepped up to plan it.
Call me tonight, I'm working until 4.
PS Wanna go?!!

Kellie traced the outline of her nose as she stared at the message. The words glared back at her, each exclamation point a tiny finger pointing and laughing. Suzanne loved exclamation points. Twenty-five years since high school. There'd never been a reunion, apparently. Not that she would have gone anyway. Cherry Weiss, the cheerleader. Pretty girl, very popular. She wouldn't even remember me, Kellie thought, not that it mattered. She hit the delete button and the message disappeared. Personal emails at work weren't necessarily forbidden, but they weren't encouraged. She touched the mute button on her phone and brought the droning speaker back to life. Outside, a police car zoomed over the bridge, red and blue lights blazing.

*

"May I have a minute, Kellie?"
She swiveled around to face Elizabeth, who stood in the doorway of her office.

4

"Of course," Kellie said, and moved a pile of papers to the side of her desk. She put forth a face of calm, but her insides were churning. Elizabeth never came to her office; if she wanted something, she summoned Kellie to her lair.

Elizabeth strode across the carpet. She was, as usual, dressed perfectly. A light brown skirt, straight and slim with not a single wrinkle in the lap. Kellie wondered how that could be – did the woman work standing up? A cropped jacket of the same shade, unbuttoned to reveal a white silk shell underneath. Two strands of large coral-colored beads around her neck. Matching pumps. Elizabeth had once confessed to an obsession with expensive shoes.

"Do you want to sit down?" Kellie remained seated, aware that her own skirt was no doubt creased.

"Ed and I would like you to come to a little dinner party at our house. A week from this Saturday, the sixth. It's the holiday weekend. Ed's invited a co-worker friend from the office and we think you two would hit it off." She smiled, and Kellie imagined Elizabeth must have had her teeth whitened recently. Her lipstick matched those beads around her neck. Elizabeth's lips were drawn back to bare her teeth. When wolves do that, it's to show dominance, Kellie thought.

She hated this. When she worked for Elizabeth in Boston, there was a woman who was always trying to fix her up, like Kellie was some kind of matchmaker's project. And now Elizabeth was doing it, no doubt with Ed's blessing. Kellie pressed her knees together under her desk. If she lied and made up an excuse, Elizabeth would know. I'm such a bad liar, Kellie said to herself. She and Ed know me too well.

"That would be lovely. Thank you, Elizabeth." Kellie smiled but couldn't bare her teeth.

"Perfect! There'll be eight of us then. His name is Bill Hopedale. Six o'clock. You know our address? 25 Clarke

Street. There won't be any place to park, so you should take a taxi."

Kellie raised her eyebrows. Elizabeth and Ed Ford lived just up the hill, next to the Brown University campus. It wouldn't be more than a ten-minute walk from where she lived downtown. She'd wear comfortable shoes, flats just in case Bill Hopedale wasn't very tall.

"I'll probably just walk," Kellie said.

Elizabeth placed her left hand, with its dazzling diamond ring, on her narrow hip. "Even the East Side isn't safe anymore, my dear. Gangs of hoodlums roaming around the campus at night, mugging college students. They've been targeting the Asian girls, you know," she added in a whisper as her eyes darted off to the side.

"Why?"

Elizabeth raised her chin. "Because they don't fight back. You'd fight back, Kellie, wouldn't you?" She didn't wait for an answer. "Don't take any chances, dear. Get a cab."

*

Kellie headed outside at lunchtime. The day was brilliant, and offices up and down the street disgorged workers. She loved that the news station was situated in the middle of everything, a short walk to the courthouse, the federal building, and her favorite coffee shop. Young men and women sat in the park, their faces tilted to the sun. Some clutched large plastic cups of iced coffee as they walked. Others relaxed at café tables set up on the sidewalks. Kellie strolled along the river's edge until she reached her bench, near the highway overpass. There was some shade there, with the sun high above a leafy canopy. She pulled out her phone and dialed Suzanne's number. It went directly to voice mail; well, Suzanne had said she'd be working until four. Kellie left a short, upbeat message and said they'd catch up later that evening. Switching off the phone, she tucked it away and leaned back.

A young man paddled a kayak down the river toward the mouth of the bay. He raised his paddle to her as he passed and Kellie lifted her hand in return. She thought about this man Bill Hopedale, this stranger she'd have to meet. Would he be as old as Ed? What will he look like? Kellie wondered how much Bill Hopedale knew about her. He worked with Ed, but she and Ed had been friends for a long time, and he respected her privacy. Still, Kellie was sure Bill had asked the usual questions: divorced, kids, family? And Ed might have said yes, no, and not anymore. Kellie bowed her head, dreading an event that was nearly two weeks in the future. There was no way out, and she hated that aspect the most.

It was time to go back to work, and as the kayaker disappeared under the overpass, Kellie turned away and walked back to the office.

2

Joe Traversa stood in front of a wall of windows and sipped his first coffee of the morning. He looked out over the ocean, flat and gray in the morning light. He used to love this time of day, but now the quiet pounded in his ears. He flipped on the television just for some background noise. For the first time in a very long time, he was alone in his own house. No Paul cooking breakfast in the kitchen. No Paul talking back to Matt Lauer. No Paul preparing his coffee: black, half a Splenda.

Joe squeezed his eyes shut and wondered how long it would take before a new routine seemed normal. He walked barefoot across the polished teak floor and sat at his desk. He put on reading glasses and checked his email. Fourteen new messages since yesterday afternoon. And nothing from Paul. Of course not. He let out a breath he didn't even realize he'd been holding. Most of these messages he'd delete without opening. He stopped at the fifth line down. Cherry Weiss. Jesus, Cherry Weiss. There's a name from the past. How in the world did she find him? Suzanne must have given her this address, the more general one, not the private one he reserved for just his closest friends. Of course, he was all over the internet; she could have found him that way, too. *Save the date for the 25-year high school reunion.* Joe leaned back in his chair and clasped his hands on his head. The big twenty-fifth. He rocked in his chair and massaged his scalp with his fingertips. I should go, he thought, just to show them all that I won. How many of them stayed behind in dinky

8

little West Alton, he wondered. Who else had the guts to leave, right after graduation? He'd bought an old Dodge Diplomat with his graduation money, packed up, and headed west. Traded one ocean for another. He recalled his parents' faces: his mother's wet and pink, his father's dry and stony. He swallowed hard, remembering how he couldn't get away from there fast enough. How each time he crossed into another state, farther away from Rhode Island, he'd let out a whoop, alone in his car.

"Maybe better to stay here on the other side of the country," Joe said out loud, forgetting for a moment that there was no one there to answer. He snapped the laptop closed and headed out for his morning run.

*

Scott Hunter could barely raise his head off the pillow. He squinted at the clock on the table beside his bed. Illuminated red numbers screamed 10:02. Well, at least he was alone. Last time he'd done shots with Will, he'd brought home some skanky girl with a pierced tongue and tattoos up and down her arm. Didn't even know her name, but there she was the next morning, smiling at him and asking for breakfast. Jeez.

He lifted his body from the lumpy mattress and walked to the window. Pulling a cord to lift the blinds, he squinted against the brilliant sunshine that blasted him. He shuffled to the kitchen, opened a cupboard, and grabbed a blue can of coffee from the shelf. It felt light. He peeled off the plastic lid and looked inside. Empty. Not even enough damn coffee. He tossed the can onto the counter. It rolled to the edge and stopped, as if knowing that falling to the floor would only result in dents and bruises.

Scott opened the refrigerator. One can of Coke, good enough. He popped the top and swigged half the contents, letting the sugar and caffeine work their way into his alcohol-soaked body. A little sharper now, he fired up the computer, an old, slow Dell. One new message. Cherry Weiss from high school. Jeez. High school reunion in November. Twenty-five years. He figured he might as well go; it'd be good to see a couple of his buddies and goof on all the girls who got fat. Will and Robbie would go. And he'd tell Will not to bring that bitch of a wife with him.

One more week until the disability check arrived. After sixteen years with the West Alton Fire Department, he'd had an accident one day on the job. No one witnessed it, but it caused Scott such tremendous back pain that he was unable to work anymore. And by law, the town of West Alton was required to pay him a tax-free pension equal to roughly forty thousand dollars. Every year. He opened his wallet and counted the bills inside. Two hundred and ten bucks should get him through the week.

He did fifty sit-ups on his living room floor, counting them down. "Twenty-eight, twenty-seven," he grunted, and cheated on the last ten.

Drinking down the rest of his Coke, he looked out his front window to the parking lot below. School was out for summer, but some of the grad students stayed around for classes. He watched a chubby girl with a blonde ponytail squeeze into a tiny white car and smiled at the familiar stirring.

Tossing the can into the trash, he scratched himself and farted.

3

Cherry Weiss wouldn't allow herself to slow down. She had a long list of things to accomplish, and she made a small checkmark next to each item as it was completed. The "save the date" emails were sent. Check. She'd found most of her classmates but there were still about a dozen for whom she couldn't find an email address. She'd plowed through social media sites trying to locate everyone, making phone calls, confirming names. It was her job as the chair of the reunion committee, which right now consisted of just her. The twenty-fifth reunion was five months away. She had so much to do. There had never been a reunion for West Alton Regional High, and Cherry was determined to pull it off. This time it was different; twenty-five years was a big milestone, and even if she had to do all the work herself, she wanted it to succeed. She just wished one or two of her classmates would have been interested in helping. Amber wrote back that she was "so freakin' busy," and Tiffany made some excuse about her parents. Since she still lived with her parents at forty-three, Cherry didn't expect much from her. Tiffany might as well still be in the tenth grade, Cherry thought with a shake of her head.

She flipped through her yearbook. She had entered each classmate's name into a spreadsheet on her computer. Columns for maiden and married names, marital status, email address, mailing address, phone number and RSVP reply. She had listed everyone who was in the yearbook, and even remembered to include Holly Tate, who left school midway through senior year to have a baby and whose senior photo was deleted by the principal.

She stared at the picture of Joe Traversa. She hoped he would attend; it would bring a little stardom to their reunion. Everyone liked Joe, and she imagined that they'd all want to see him now that he was famous. She pictured some of her classmates telling their friends that they went to high school with Joe Traversa, the Oscar-winning movie director. Quickly she made a note to see if she could get press coverage, should he attend.

Cherry wanted to right things in her life. If anything, finding the lump in her breast had taught her to take nothing for granted. Mend a fence when possible. She wanted to be the person who brought her classmates together. It was a shame they'd never had a reunion. The class president, Ian Winters, was serving time in prison for defrauding dozens of investors out of their retirement savings. No one else had stepped forward, not any of the other class officers.

"Mom, I'm home!" The familiar call of Niket interrupted her thoughts. Cherry pushed away from the computer and started downstairs. Nick would be hungry, no doubt, and Cherry always wanted to be there for him when he came home from school. She didn't like to think too much about the future, about what it might be like for Nick to come home to nothing, to an empty house. But sometimes the darker thoughts invaded and she couldn't will them away.

"Nick-nack!" She held her arms out to her only child, who still let her hug him. Momma's boy, she thought with a smile, just the way I like it. She held him at arm's length and surveyed the beautiful boy in front of her. He favored his father with thick dark hair and large black eyes, but he had her lips. When he smiled, tears sprang to her eyes and Cherry blinked hard. She didn't want Nick to see her get emotional. She and Bud had told Nick about the lump two days ago, but they were upbeat and optimistic, hoping to convince him it was so early that there was no cause for concern. In Nick's eyes, though, Cherry could tell. He was scared.

"Are you hungry, sweetheart?" She grinned at him. "Silly question, right?"

"Mom, I can make my own snack," he said. "Let me get something for you," he added.

"Absolutely not!" Cherry cried. She would not be waited on by her son. "I'll heat up a samosa for each of us, okay? It'll just take a minute, and we'll eat together. Then you can do your homework."

Cherry wrapped two samosas in a damp paper towel and placed them in the microwave. She set the timer and took a small bowl of mango chutney from the refrigerator. While Nick washed his hands in the bathroom down the hall, Cherry placed the chutney and two glasses of water on the table.

The microwave chimed. Cherry swayed once and everything went black.

4

Her phone rang precisely at seven o'clock. Kellie checked the caller ID and saw Suzanne's name. She smiled. *Suzanne knows I like to watch the nightly news,* she thought.

"Hello, my friend." Kellie picked up the remote and silenced the television.

"Hey, Kell," Suzanne said. "How's it going?"

Kellie put her on speaker and set the phone on the kitchen counter while she took a wine glass from the cupboard.

"Oh, you know, typical Monday. Let me just pour a glass of wine." She retrieved a bottle from the refrigerator door and pulled the cork. Filling the glass halfway, she set the bottle on the counter next to the phone.

"Wish I could be there with you," Suzanne said. "I've got a Sam Adams in my hand right now."

"Well, cheers," Kellie said, tapping her glass against the wine bottle so her friend could hear it. She brought the phone and her glass to the living room and settled into her favorite chair.

"Did you have a bad day?"

Kellie exhaled. "It was okay, for a Monday. The usual stuff. And, of course, your email." She sipped her wine while she waited for Suzanne's response.

"I know, can you believe it? I'm assuming you didn't get a message from her. She wouldn't know how to find you anyway."

"Suze, she probably doesn't even remember me. I wouldn't expect her to. Cherry Weiss the cheerleader, right? Pretty, dark hair?" Kellie remembered her. She had a slew of friends. Kellie pictured them standing near a bank of lockers, dressed in their cheerleader outfits, giggling at boys. She didn't think Cherry Weiss would have any idea she even existed. There wouldn't have been any reason; they were worlds apart. "A high school reunion. Come on, not in a million years."

"Well, I don't know," Suzanne said slowly.

"It's different for you. You had friends." Kellie realized that came out sounding whiny, not at all how she'd intended. Suzanne only had a few friends, and Kellie was one of them. Plus Joe Traversa, who was famous in Hollywood now. She saw him on television last year, when he won the Oscar.

She imagined Cherry Weiss, yearbook in hand, tracking down as many classmates as she could. Kellie didn't have a picture taken for the yearbook. She avoided cameras as much as possible back then. Plus, she never would have asked her mother to buy photographs. What was the point? Cherry probably didn't even think about Kellie, especially with no picture to remind her.

"Twenty-five years, Kell. How did that happen?" Kellie heard Suzanne take a gulp. "So you'd never even consider going, not even with me?"

"Are you serious? Why would I ever go back to that place? It's bad enough I had to come back to Rhode Island."

Suzanne's voice was small. "Well, I'm glad you're closer."

"Well, of course. I'm glad I'm closer to you, too. But high school? No thanks."

"I understand," Suzanne said. "It's just, well, it's the twenty-fifth. I think Joe Traversa might even come back."

"Really? Have you spoken with him?" Kellie traced a finger along her cheek.

"Mostly just emails. We keep in touch. I never thought he'd want to come back, either. I mean, he had a rough time in high school, but I think he's considering it. This one time."

"He was so well liked! And now he has an Oscar." Everyone liked Joey in high school, Kellie thought. Funny, self-deprecating Joe Traversa, famous, living in Los Angeles, open about his sexuality. A very good-looking man. A couple of months ago there was a feature about him in the newspaper, a "local boy hits it big" retrospective. The other station snagged an interview with him when one of their reporters was out in Los Angeles. Elizabeth was not happy about that.

Kellie remembered the piece. The reporter talked about Joey being a model for years, then that he started directing when he was in his thirties, and finally won his first Academy Award for directing *A Little Green*. It was a good movie. But Kellie couldn't imagine why he'd ever want to return to West Alton.

"Can you come down for a visit this weekend? Skye leaves Friday for Stockbridge, and Jake's pulling so much overtime, he's staying in Groton with a bunch of his buddies. We could have a sleepover!" Kellie knew Suzanne; she hated to be alone.

"How about I drive down Saturday afternoon?" Suzanne lived in Mystic, a sweet little Connecticut town that was famous once for its shipbuilding. It was touristy, with a maritime museum, an aquarium, a seaport, and Mystic Pizza, the restaurant made famous in that Julia Roberts movie.

"I'll make lasagna," she offered.

"And I'll bring wine," Kellie said. Just Suzanne and me, again, Kellie thought. She hadn't been down to visit her friend since she'd moved to Rhode Island from Boston. It's better without Jake, anyway. She knew Jake was uncomfortable around her. Suzanne had probably told him everything about her life.

She hung up the phone and thought about tomorrow. Her closet was filled with clothes, and she fingered a skirt patterned with blue and green flowers. Kellie remembered the tie-dyed skirt her mother had made for her. No one wore tie-dye in 1988, but then again, no one had a mother like Barbara Campbell. Forever stuck in 1969, and nearly twenty years after Woodstock, she still dressed like a hippie. Another memory surfaced, rising up from the depths of her subconscious. Kellie sat cross-legged on the floor of her bedroom, letting the recollection wrap around her like a warm embrace. Her mother had finally decided to answer Kellie's questions about her father. As they huddled together under a heavy quilt, while Adam slept at the other end of the trailer, Kellie learned about the man who had fathered her.

Barbara Ann Campbell was raised in a strict household, but the summer between her freshman and sophomore years at Skidmore, she defied her parents and joined up with three of her college classmates who were headed to the three-day festival in upstate New York. Amidst the mud and drugs, she hooked up with a man named Arthur Blunt and Kellie was conceived in a leaky, smoky tent during the Jimi Hendrix concert.

"But you never married him?" Twelve-year-old Kellie searched her mother's eyes.

"No, it wasn't like that," her mother answered. Her eyes were miles away, somewhere on a dairy farm in Bethel, New York. "We were in the moment, living for the music, being one soul in two bodies."

"Well, didn't he want to marry you when you told him you were going to have me?"

Barbara Campbell stroked her daughter's hair, pushing it back from her forehead. She began humming a tune about golden rainbows.

"I didn't tell him, Kellie. I never wanted to obligate him. He was a free spirit. He'd stayed on the farm, and I assumed he was still there."

Kellie leaned back from her mother. "But my name is Blunt and your name is Campbell," she asserted.

"Well, even if I had married your father, Kellie, I would have kept my own name. It's *my* name."

"Okay." Kellie frowned but let the conversation end there. She wished her name was Kellie Campbell instead of Kellie Blunt, because that horrible boy Scott Hunter had started calling her a nasty name that rhymed with Blunt. Nothing bad rhymed with Campbell, she was pretty sure of it.

Kellie stood up and looked into her closet. Her parents were two teenagers, wet, muddy, and most likely stoned when they created her. She shut her eyes and hummed the song she remembered so well, about the golden rainbows. When she opened her eyes, there was the skirt with the blue and green flowers. She hung it back on the closet rod and selected a pale gray lightweight suit instead.

*

"Mom!" Cherry heard her son's voice, distant but getting louder. She felt his hand on her shoulder and opened her eyes to see Nick's face come into focus; it was twisted with concern. Cherry blinked twice and struggled to sit up.

"Mom, take it easy," said Nick. "What happened?" He increased pressure on her shoulder to keep her from trying to sit up too fast.

"Honey, I just fainted. I really should have eaten earlier," she said to her son, hoping he'd believe her. But she could see the fear in his eyes. "Come on, help me up, Nick-nack. Let's have a samosa."

Nick was getting so big; in the past year he'd grown three inches. His strong arms lifted Cherry to her feet and guided her to a chair at the table. Nick retrieved the warm samosas from the microwave and set them on the table.

"Mom, it's really important that you eat," Nick said. "Try not to go so fast. You never stop, you know," he added, pulling his black eyebrows together in a frown.

Cherry couldn't help but smile at her boy. Over the coming months, would he become the caregiver? No, she thought firmly, he has school. He needed to focus on his studies, maybe start to date. He'd begin driving lessons soon. There was so much ahead for Nick. And Cherry couldn't bear to think about not being around to see it.

5

June 25 – 158 days to go

Scott Hunter's days were pretty much all the same. Wake up, coffee, work out, shower, eat, nap, go out. Once in a while, not often enough, get laid. He was bored out of his mind and he hated always having to look over his shoulder. The local politicians were talking about the deficit, having to raise taxes. Just last week in the diner, where he sat at the counter eating an omelet and toast, a couple of old guys in a booth behind him were saying the town was going broke because of the pensions for municipal workers.

"Used to be you couldn't get rich workin' civil service," one of them said. "Now look at 'em. They're driving friggin' German cars. Since when does a retired cop have enough money for a Mercedes?"

Scott almost swiveled around, but he stopped himself. Couple of idiots. He couldn't wait to move to Florida, away from these stupid people. He'd lived in West Alton his entire life, and finally he was getting ready to leave this town. Move to Florida. Prettier girls down there. And no tax on his car.

He shoveled the remainder of his omelet in his mouth and washed it down with coffee. There wouldn't be any fun this weekend, he knew that much. Not with Tara coming to stay. He didn't even know what to do with her anymore. Besides, she never seemed too happy to spend the weekend with him, but he guessed that Laurinda was just as glad to pawn her off. At least they'd only had the one, and his other two kids, the boys, were off on their own and living out of state. Not that they ever invited him out for a visit or anything. Hell, he'd never even met his grandson. But they always cashed his checks right away, didn't they?

Scott pulled some bills from his wallet to pay his tab, and there was Tara staring back at him, a two-by-three-inch photo of his fourteen-year-old daughter, looking like a streetwalker in heavy eye makeup. He remembered how hot Laurinda had looked the first time he saw her. He was still married to Carlene, but neither of them was really into the marriage anymore. Still, he'd taken his wife to that Italian restaurant for their anniversary, the one down by the beach, with the old-fashioned red-and-white checkered tablecloths. Laurinda was their waitress, and she'd been pouring it on for him all night. He'd noticed, the extra button undone on her blouse, the way she leaned over the table to serve plates of linguine and red clam sauce. He'd tucked a fifty-dollar tip and his cell phone number inside the little credit card folder. She'd called him the next day and by the following weekend they were together.

Before his divorce was even final, Laurinda was pregnant, and Tara was born before they'd had a chance to get married. At first he suspected she'd set him up; then he was sure of it. They split up when Tara was eight, and Laurinda remarried within six months. Now Tara was fourteen, and she scared the shit out of Scott sometimes.

*

June 27 – 156 days to go

Joe had a late-morning meeting with two of the studio executives. He never scheduled meetings before eleven. There was still time for a run on the beach and a shower. Best to keep busy, not think about Paul, where he might be, who he might have met already. He hadn't left a forwarding address when he left, just that note. Five lines written in his careful handwriting: *"You've given me more than I deserved. But it's time for me to move on. I can't keep taking, and I need to find out who I am without you. We had a great run! And I do love you, JoJo."*

The photograph still stood on his desk, next to his Academy award. Joe stared at the photo, remembering the day last September, on David Herzog's yacht. In the picture, Joe's head inclined toward Paul's, and both of them were grinning. *What a good-looking couple we were. Better days,* Joe thought. *I hope he's happy. No, I don't. I hope he's as miserable as I am.* He picked up the photo and looked at it closely, as if there was a hidden clue that would explain why Paul left. He considered dumping it in the trash bin. *Not yet,* he said to himself as he set it back in its place. *Not quite yet.*

Joe laced up his running shoes and slipped his driver's license in the zip pocket of his shorts. Paul had taught him that. He locked the door behind him and headed to the beach.

*

June 29 – 154 days to go

Kellie arrived at Suzanne's house on Saturday afternoon. It was a straight line down Route 95 and there wasn't much traffic, to her surprise. As she drove past the exit for West Alton, she kept her eyes on the road, until the exit sign and ramp were behind her.

Suzanne's house was set back inland, along the Pequot Brook, a tall, hundred-year-old house with gables. The roof was missing some shingles, she noticed. And the front porch seemed to sag in the middle. Kellie wondered how safe the house was; old houses needed constant attention and repair. The rhododendrons were in bloom, their deep purple-red blossoms spattered against the clapboard exterior. A detached garage stood off to one side, independent of the house. Suzanne said she used to make pottery in the garage, but the wheel sat alone now.

Kellie turned into the gravel driveway and parked next to an old Ford truck with rust speckling the back bumper. The side door to the house was open, and she called out "Suzie!" through the screen. A voice called back, "It's open!" Kellie hoisted her bags to shoulder and hip, and used two fingers to pull open the door. She noticed a small hole in the screen at eye level. Someone should mend that hole, she thought. Mosquitos will come in.

She walked through a mud room cluttered with dusty snow boots and parkas. A large wicker basket sat on the floor, filled with woolen hats and scarves, and a pair of sky-blue mittens with white snowflakes on them. Kellie wiped sweat from her forehead and stepped into the kitchen. Suzanne turned from the counter, her hands twisted up in a cotton towel. Her hair, more gray than blonde now, was short, and earrings dangled against her neck. Even without makeup, Suzanne looked the same as she did in high school. The only thing different was her hair.

"Kell's bells," she said, opening her arms.

Kellie set her overnight bag on the floor and laid a green cloth shopping bag on the kitchen counter. She hugged Suzanne hard and realized it had been a very long time since she'd had physical contact with anyone. It felt good. Suzanne peeked inside the bag and grinned. "You made brownies!" She clapped her hands together. "I made vegetable lasagna, is that okay?"

"You think I baked? The brownies are store-bought. Hurry up and open the wine," she said.

*

Later that evening, full from dinner and mellowed by chianti, Kellie pulled her legs up and tucked them under herself on the sofa.

"You look like you have a secret," Suzanne said from the chair. She tipped her wine glass up and drank down what was left, then reached for the bottle, topping off both glasses.

Kellie rolled her eyes. "I have a blind date next Saturday. My boss set it up. I couldn't say no." She took a deep breath and let her lungs expand. She released the breath slowly. Wasn't that supposed to be calming?

"You couldn't say no? Why, because you work for her? She shouldn't have done that. If you don't want to go, make something up."

"What was I going to do? You've never met her. It's just a stupid dinner party." She picked up her glass again. "Besides, I'd like to see Ed. It's just that I can never see him without seeing her."

"Well, maybe this guy will be nice. What do you know about him?"

"He works with Ed. Bill something. Hopedale." Kellie felt a little fuzzy and the bottle was empty. She wondered if they should open another. Maybe.

"Bill Hopeful," Suzanne said and they both laughed. "I'd love to see you meet someone good, Kell. A normal guy."

"Ha. Might have missed the boat on that one." A thickness in her throat startled her.

Suzanne swirled around the ruby liquid in her glass. "Maybe not. Have hope. Have Hopedale." She looked up at Kellie and giggled. Like they were teenagers again, whispering about boys. "We're definitely opening another bottle," she said.

She rose to her feet, wobbled, righted herself, and asked, "Should we? Are we too wasted now? I always think if I get too drunk, what if one of us needed to drive or something. What if someone broke in and I couldn't find the phone? Jake's never here." She made a face. "Even when he's here, he's not here," she said in a quieter voice. She steadied herself against the back of the sofa. "I hate the thought of Skye moving out. Did I tell you, she's doing this veterinary camp in Stockbridge? I told you, right? She'll probably love it and want to live there. Then it'll be just Jake and me, Kell, and we never seem to have anything to talk about. He doesn't want to hear about my job, says it's too sad to hear about old people dying. And I don't want to hear about his. It's boring." Suzanne looked like she might cry, but she didn't. She just stood between the living room and the kitchen, swaying.

"Let's not open another bottle," Kellie said. "Sit down, I'll get the brownies." She walked carefully into the kitchen. Better not let her drink any more tonight, Kellie thought. Poor Suzanne, married to that schmuck. She knew the feeling, twice.

There was a noise outside, like the crackling of sticks underfoot. The side door had been left unlocked the entire time. Now Kellie walked back into the mud room and closed it, turning the deadbolt and checking to make sure it was secure. How could Suzanne sleep upstairs alone in this old house, she wondered. She returned to the kitchen and peered through the window above the sink. Nothing but woods and blackness. Kellie picked up the plate of brownies in one hand and took her purse in the other. She reminded herself not to leave it in the kitchen. She'd keep her cell phone next to her in the bed. Better yet, she'd just sleep with Suzanne.

6

Joe had wrapped shooting most of the new film. It was a risky move, veering away from the typical biopics he'd been directing for the past ten years, but he'd loved the script for this drama and knew he could make it work on the screen, especially with Roberto Ozuna as his leading man. Ozuna was just twenty-three, but had caught everyone's attention in his debut film last year, and Joe could see he was a rising star. Resembling a younger Enrique Iglesias, Roberto had it all, and his heavy Spanish accent made him even sexier to his adoring fans. The tabloids followed him everywhere, and Roberto seemed to revel in the attention, which made Joe nervous. A kid in Hollywood with a lot of attention and a lot of money could go wrong very quickly.

After years of working hard, making contacts, and keeping promises, Joe Traversa was successful and well-respected in the industry. And he had more money than he'd ever imagined. His aging parents lived in Miami Beach now, and Joe had bought the condo they lived in. Well, if he was being honest, he'd bought it for his mother, in spite of his father's objections that they could damn well pay for their own housing. Joe's house on Malibu Road was worth ten times more than what he'd paid for it in 2001, when he'd purchased it from a washed-up actress who'd blown through her money and was desperate to sell. Joe had put a lot into refurbishing the house, and it was one of the most beautiful homes in Malibu. Gorgeous. And empty. Paul had breathed life and energy into the house and made it a home for the two of them. He loved entertaining, more than Joe did, but Paul could turn a small dinner party into an event that was talked about for weeks.

Joe hated the quiet. Used to be, he'd come home to Paul, and music, and tantalizing smells coming from the kitchen. Paul loved salsa music, and Joe couldn't stand to listen to it anymore. One of the scenes in the new movie called for Roberto to practice dancing in front of a mirror, and as Joe sat in his director's chair, watching Roberto shimmy and twirl in tight black briefs, he had to close his eyes to the beauty that made his chest hurt.

He was considering a return trip to Rhode Island for his high school reunion. He still wasn't sure about it, but Suzanne was so happy with the idea that Joe knew he'd disappoint her if he didn't go. The memory of his high school years still caused pain, even after twenty-five years. He knew he looked good, probably a lot better than those Neanderthals back east who had likely lost their hair and grown beer bellies. He'd love to see Suzanne again. She was his best friend back in high school. And *she* was best friends with that poor Kellie Blunt. It's what he loved about Suzanne: that she could always see past one's external flaws and imperfections to the beauty of what was inside. Most teenaged kids weren't capable of that. She loved me for me, thought Joe, and she really did love Kellie. Joe had tried to be friendly to Kellie, but she was so shy. She would never even look in his eyes, and after a few attempts at conversation in the school's cafeteria, he'd given up. Joe wondered about Kellie Blunt, where she was now, what she was doing. Suzanne would know.

Here I am, thought Joe, single again after five years. He wouldn't bring a date to a high school reunion in a small provincial Rhode Island town anyway – they could never handle it. He shivered as he remembered that night in April, the night before the senior play opened. How he almost didn't make it. How his mother, his angel, convinced him to go onstage and give the best performance he was capable of. He did, and no one even knew about the previous night's horror, except the ones who were there.

Joe wondered how many of his classmates were gay and just didn't know it, or weren't able to find their truth back then. He remembered reading about that kid Aaron Fricke in Cumberland, who took a guy to the prom. He had to go to court. Joe knew he would never have had the guts to do something like that. When the Fricke story came out, he was only ten, but he'd heard about it forever. Joe was supposed to take Suzanne to the prom, but with what had happened, he just couldn't do it. He'd let her down, and yet she was so understanding. She didn't even know why, not until months later, when, a week before her wedding, they'd shared a bottle of wine and smoked a joint, and he told her the whole, horrible story.

His high school reunion. Twenty-five years. He shook his head in amazement that so much time had passed. If he was going to go to only one reunion, it might as well be the twenty-fifth. By the time the fiftieth rolled around, he'd be decrepit. He opened his laptop and began typing a message to Suzanne.

*

Scott was about three miles away from his apartment when his car just slowed down and stopped. He had exited the highway and was on one of the seldom used back roads. West Alton was still rural, still called 'the sticks' by most people who lived in and around the cities. Scott had lived there all his life, and he knew every square inch of the area.

He pounded the steering wheel and cursed to the windshield. The car's death didn't come as much of a surprise, or at least it shouldn't have. He'd put close to 200,000 miles on it, but still. Four fuckin' miles from home, he thought. And Tara showing up that afternoon.

He stepped out of the car and locked the doors. Unless he got lucky and someone picked him up, he'd be walking for another hour. He glared at the darkening sky. "You'd better not fuckin' rain," he threatened with a raised fist. The clouds rumbled in reply. He pulled out his cell phone. "Shit!" he yelled out loud when he saw it wasn't charged. And his charger was back in his apartment. "Why me? Why do these things always happen to me?"

As he trudged up the road, Scott's breathing became more labored. To the right he spotted a chalet-style home, set back from the road, just visible through the thick green underbrush and leafy trees. He didn't know who lived there, but there was an enormous black dog lying on the gravel driveway, and he wasn't about to try his luck with ninety pounds of fur and fangs. Dogs didn't care much for Scott, and the feeling was mutual. Farther up the road, on the left, was an unpaved path, wide enough for one car but not two. It wasn't even a named road, just a shortcut created over the years by cars driving through the fields to get somewhere else, but Scott knew it well. He used to drive through on his way home from school, skimming his Mustang past fields and pastures. He'd bring girls out there at night and get as far as he could with them, parked off the path and camouflaged by trees. The cops never bothered to come out there. Back when he was working, he'd use the shortcut to get home after his shift ended. Sometimes he'd have a girl with him, and a case of beer in the back. He'd drink cans of Miller Lite and toss the empties out the window. Sometimes they'd pass a fat joint back and forth, and eventually he'd make his move on her. Where were all those girls now, he wondered.

He kept walking, another mile, past an old abandoned trailer that squatted low in the field. It was mostly obscured now, left to rust and rot in the sun. Tall grass grew around it, and only the roof was visible. If the economy ever improved, someone would buy up the land and build prefab McMansions to newly-rich city assholes who wanted to live in the country. Then they'd cry for a drive-through coffee place on the corner, a pharmacy that was open twenty-four hours a day, a fast food joint for their brats. Hopefully he'd be long gone by then.

Scott stopped to catch his breath and stared at the trailer. He felt something hit his shoulder. Turning his head, he saw a caterpillar crawling down his arm. He flicked it off and looked up to see the trees were filled with white web-like masses. The gypsy moths. He walked faster. The rumbling from the sky grew louder.

Raindrops splattered on his face. "Ah fuck," he muttered. He tried to jog down the abandoned path, knowing it would bring him to the intersection and the road where his apartment complex stood. He'd jogged just a few steps and had to bend in half to suck air into his lungs. The dirt road was lined with tall oaks and maples that camouflaged the sky. Caterpillars were all over the place, some flattened, some still inching their way to the woods. The rain was light, not a downpour at least, and thirty minutes later he finally came to the end of the path. Now it was just another ten minutes' walk down Corn Maze Valley Road. Scott cast one more glance behind him, half-expecting the ugly old trailer to roar to life and chase him.

*

Back home, he called Will. "Bud, I need a favor."

"What's up?"

"My fuckin' car just died, man. And Tara's coming this afternoon. I need wheels."

"Hang on a sec." Scott heard Will's voice, muffled, and an unintelligible reply from his wife. Their voices rose, but Scott couldn't make out what they were saying. Finally Will came back on the line.

"Alright, you can use mine this weekend." He lowered his voice to a whisper. "Now I gotta take Ellen to that fancy French place in the city for dinner tonight, man. You owe me."

Scott laughed. "Bring it by as soon as you can. I gotta get food for the kid. Hey, brother, thanks."

"Yeah, yeah," said Will before clicking off.

Scott moved around the small apartment, straightening pillows, brushing away a cobweb from a lamp. The rain did nothing to wash away the humidity, and he was soaked in sweat. He pulled open the sliding door to the deck and waited for a breeze that never came.

Laurinda would drop off Tara at four. His fourteen-year-old didn't sound too enthusiastic when they talked on the phone yesterday. No sex for Scotty this weekend, he thought, reflecting on the craziness with Liz earlier in the week. She was insatiable, that girl. Even liked it a little rough. He'd left a few bruises on her wrists and ankles, but she'd probably wear them like badges. That was Liz.

Scott figured he'd take Tara to Chili's and even bring her to see that stupid movie she'd been whining about wanting to see. The Grand Am was dead, and he'd need something. He called his buddy Hank at Tri-Town.

"Hey, Scottso. What's happening, my man?"

"My fuckin' car died, Hank, that's what happening. On Babcock Road. It's done. I need something that'll get me around. And don't try to sell me something new."

He heard Hank whistle through his teeth on the other end.

"I got a LaCrosse, '09, just brought in last week. Some old lady in Danielson owned it. She dies, the kids bring it to me in trade. Only 14,000 miles on it. I'll let you take it for, say, fourteen."

Scott let a few seconds pass. "Twelve."

"Jesus, Scott, it's worth at least fourteen."

"And I'm your friend, Hank," Scott replied evenly.

Hank muttered an expletive and Scott smiled. "Fine. Twelve."

"I'll be there today if I can," he said and hung up.

He heard a car's horn and looked out the window. Will parked his car in an empty space and hopped out. Ellen was in the Jeep, idling in the lot. Scott called out, "Will! Hold up!" He ran barefoot down the stairs and out the door. He twisted his body to wave to Ellen through the window, and she glared back at him. She hates me, he said to himself. Bitch.

"Hey, Hank at Tri-Town has a car for me. Can we just go there instead? Then you can have your car back."

Will rolled his eyes before leaning in the passenger window to speak to his wife. She drove away without a word and Will turned back to Scott.

"Well, I still have to take her to dinner."

Scott laughed. "Buy her a nice meal, buddy, maybe you'll get lucky tonight."

"Yeah, luckier than you."

"Fuck you, let's go."

*

The doorbell rang. Scott opened the door and saw Laurinda's white Chevy Tahoe tear away. Like she couldn't get away fast enough. The only reason she had a Tahoe was because she married a contractor. Scott bet he was on the take, too.

"Hey, beautiful," he said, turning back to Tara. Man, she looked so grown-up. Her hair hung straight and shiny past her shoulders, and she had little doorknob breasts beneath a pink tee shirt that had the word 'luscious' written across the front. She wore way too much make-up for a girl her age, Scott thought, wondering why Laurinda allowed it. Her eyes were rimmed in black and she looked ridiculous. But he kept his mouth shut.

Tara's mouth contorted. "Oh my God, Dad, it's so freakin' hot in here! Turn on the air conditioner!" Scott thought she might cry, and he had a flicker of hope that she'd change her mind and call her mother, saying she couldn't possibly stay in her father's hot-as-hell apartment.

"It's on, baby. Takes a lot to cool the whole place down. Don't worry, it'll be fine tonight, and you can sleep in the bedroom," he soothed. "I don't mind sleeping out on the porch." Tara's raccoon eyes scowled at him. "We'll be out of here anyway. I thought we'd go to your favorite restaurant, then I'd take you to that movie you want to see." He raised his eyebrows in hopeful anticipation. "Is it a date?"

Tara stuck her lower lip out, just like she used to do when she was a baby. "I saw the movie yesterday with Taylor and Bailee."

Scott felt a pounding in his temples. "Well, there's bound to be another movie, right?"

She shook her pretty little head. "Let's go to the mall instead. There's an Applebee's."

Scott rolled his shoulders, and wondered if he could get a massage at the mall. Tara was looking at him the same way Laurinda looked at him that first year of their marriage. Like he was an idiot. He saw Laurinda in her face, her lips, those baby blue eyes ringed in black. Laurinda let his daughter look like a fuckin' whore, he thought. And that shirt. *Luscious?* What kind of shirt is that for a fourteen year old to be wearing? He couldn't wait to move to Florida. He'd send child support, which is all either of them wanted, anyway.

"Okay, sweetheart. By the time we get back here, it'll be cooler, I promise."

"Whatever. The mall sells air conditioners, Dad. You should buy another one."

7

June 30 – 153 days to go

They were still alive the next morning. Kellie had slept next to Suzanne in the big bed, in Jake's spot, and Suzanne never moved all night. At sunrise, Kellie had heard Suzanne rise, but kept her eyes closed, hoping for maybe another hour of sleep. With the two bedroom windows open for air, she listened to the sounds from the woods. Chirps and pips and hoots. Who the hell would choose to live in the woods? No wonder she hadn't slept much last night, even with all that wine in her system.

Kellie slid out of bed and tucked her bare feet into the sandals she'd worn yesterday. She didn't like to be barefoot, except in her own house. She stopped in the bathroom before making her way downstairs, to the welcome smell of coffee brewing.

"Morning," she called from the bottom step as she rounded the doorway and entered the big kitchen. Outside the window was nothing but green, leafy and verdant and thick and alive. She couldn't even see the sky through all that green. So green it made her eyes hurt.

She pulled out a chair and sat at the table, a thick slab of blond wood with nicks and scratches on the surface. Suzanne handed her a mug of hot coffee and pushed a bowl of sugar packets and a carton of soy creamer toward her. Kellie looked at the bowl. Sugar packets in all colors: white, brown, yellow, pink, and blue. She pulled a brown one up and tore it open, pouring large golden sugar crystals into her coffee. Ah, coffee. Too much wine last night.

"Is this from Whole Foods, too?" Suzanne's knife hovered above the coffee cake.

Kellie nodded for a piece and replied, "I hope it's good."

"Of course it's good, everything they do is great," she said. "I don't bake anymore, either. Jake's been on a no-carbs kick lately. Salad and chicken, that's all he ever wants."

They sat in comfortable silence, listening to the birds call to each other in their indecipherable language. Clearing out the fuzziness from last night's wine, Kellie nibbled on a piece of cinnamon cake and knew she could never give up carbs.

"So you really wouldn't go to this reunion, even if Joe and I went?" Suzanne peeked at Kellie over her mug.

Kellie set down her fork. "Seriously, why? No one besides you even knew I existed. Okay, Joe, too, but only because of you. Not one person would care if I went or not. And I don't mean to sound whiny, because I'm okay with it. I didn't know them, and they didn't know me."

"I know you don't care about them. Just come with us. Kell, you look like a completely different person. No one would even recognize you. No one," she added with emphasis, and Kellie met her gaze.

"Ha. Yeah, I'd go incognito." Kellie scraped up the last bit of coffee cake from her plate.

"Well, that might be fun." Kellie raised her eyebrows at Suzanne, who shrugged in response. "I'm just saying. You go by Kellie Campbell these days. You don't have to be Kellie Blunt. It'd be like the fly on a wall, you know? You could observe."

Kellie wrapped her fingers around the tall mug. She bet Suzanne had made this mug, and imagined her straddling the pottery wheel in the garage, molding the wet clay into this vessel. "If I had been someone else in high school, I mean, someone popular, with friends, not someone who was ridiculed for the way I looked, the way I dressed, maybe I'd want to go, just for fun. But I don't care what these people have done with their lives, no more than they care about me. Listen, I could still spend time with you two when he flies out."

Suzanne poured more coffee for both of them. "Are you worried about seeing Scott Hunter? Is that why?"

"You just said no one would recognize me. So why should that bother me?"

Suzanne lifted her thin shoulders up to her ears and dropped them. "You haven't seen him in twenty-five years. Maybe seeing him again would stir up old memories."

Kellie raised the mug and buried her face in it. She took a long time before setting it back on the table. When she looked up at Suzanne, her friend's eyes were full of tears.

"Don't cry, Suzie. I don't. I don't waste my tears on him."

"I didn't mean to upset you, Kell. You know that, right?"

Kellie picked up the plates and mugs and brought them to the sink. Looking out the window and into the tangle of green, she said, "I wouldn't mind seeing Joe Traversa again. When he flies in for the reunion, we'll get together." She rinsed the dishes and laid them on a drying rack. Suzanne didn't have a dishwasher in the old house.

"You want to do something today? Head into town?"

"Maybe just the bookstore. Then I have to get back." She didn't understand why, but she needed to leave Suzanne's house and return to her fortress. And when she drove away from Mystic, she avoided the highway and that exit sign to West Alton.

*

July 1 – 152 days to go

Cherry's biopsy was scheduled for eight o'clock, first thing in the morning. She'd be home by the afternoon, they told her. Bud had his brother-in-law run the restaurant over the weekend, so the family could spend some time together. The Kashmir Grille was open every day. Used to be, long ago, restaurants would be closed on Monday, but they couldn't afford to do that anymore. Cherry's sister Gwen arrived Sunday night and moved into the spare bedroom.

"You're an angel, you know that?" Cherry had said as she made the bed. Gwen laid neatly folded piles of cotton underwear inside the top drawer of their mother's antique dresser.

"Come on, this helps me, too. I needed to get away." Gwen's hair hung in front of her face, and Cherry couldn't see her expression.

"Well, I'm glad to have you here, sis." She fluffed the pillows and smoothed out the bedspread. Gwen *was* a godsend, Cherry thought. Of her three sisters, Cherry was closest to Gwen. Gwen was two years older, and Naomi and Monica had ten years on Gwen. All four of the Weiss girls got along, but Naomi and Monica both lived in North Carolina, just a few miles apart. Plus, Gwen was Nick's godmother.

Just a routine biopsy. That's what Dr. Sing had said. Dr. Sing reminded her of the actor John Lone, from *The Last Emperor*. That movie came out her junior year, Cherry recalled. 1987. She and a guy named Bryan saw it together, at the new movie theatre in Pocasset, but she remembered not seeing much of the movie. Cherry smiled at the memory, the two of them sitting in the back row, in the dark, Bryan's hand under her sweater. On her breast. She laid her hand on her chest, where his had been. He'd worshipped her breasts.

At the last appointment, Dr. Sing explained about the stages, the options: chemo, radiation, surgery. Cherry couldn't possibly absorb and remember everything he told her. She had brochures: "Understanding Metastatic Breast Cancer." "Your Guide to the Breast Cancer Pathology Report." "Exercises after Breast Surgery." But this was just a biopsy.

"Cherry!" Bud called from downstairs.

"I'm ready, Budhil," Cherry said, using her husband's full name. "Let's get this thing over with."

"I'll be waiting here," said Gwen. She wiped her hands against her jeans before giving her sister a hug.

"No worries," Cherry whispered into Gwen's hair. "Nick likes to eat something when he gets home from school." She pulled away and swiped a finger under each eye.

"You'll be back by then, Cher. Have Bud take you for breakfast after you're done."

Cherry nodded and descended the staircase. She linked her arm through Bud's and they walked out to the car. Gwen stood in the open doorway and held her hand up, waving. Cherry raised her hand in return until the car had pulled away and she could no longer see her sister.

*

July 3 – 150 days to go

Joe Traversa booked a flight from Los Angeles to Miami for the Tuesday before Thanksgiving. He figured he'd spend the holiday with his parents, for once, and fly up to Providence the following day. He typed out a quick message to Suzanne to let her know. He hoped she still wanted to go; if not, there was no reason to go to Rhode Island.

To: *Suzanne Fitch*
From: *Joe Traversa (personal)*
Date: *July 3, 2013*

Re: Reunion and travel plans

Hey sweetie, I booked a flight to PVD. Arriving 11/29 (day after T-day with the folks in FL). Looking at Whaler's Inn (close to you?). Please say you still want to go with me. We could be so fabulous together! Did you talk to Kellie?
Think about it. Love to you and the fam. JT

He hit 'send' and closed the laptop. Tomorrow he'd check his messages, but for now, he needed to get out of the house. It was just too damned big. Even his footsteps echoed the emptiness. There was no work until next week, after the holiday.

Joe pulled on an old ball cap and aviator sunglasses, his typical disguise. In LA, no one cared. At 42, he was tall and lean, tanned and blond. He blended in with the beautiful people and no one would recognize him anyway. The tourists were always on the lookout for movie stars, not movie directors. With the day ahead of him, he thought about what Paul hated to do, where he loathed to go. Chinatown. There! He'd go to Chinatown, visit some herbal shops, art galleries, antique stores. Maybe lunch at the Empress Pavilion. Somewhere he wouldn't have to think about Paul, or run into him.

Joe was often told he had it all. Good looks, a successful career, now an Academy Award. And loads of money. He usually just smiled when he heard those things. Good looks are just a combination of genes. A successful career? He worked hard at it. Same with the Oscar. And the money? He couldn't help that he was paid so well; that was the business. There were plenty of lean years behind him, and he never lost sight of the fact that it could turn in an instant. What mattered more was having someone to share it all with. He thought he had that with Paul.

He strolled around Chinatown and saw couples holding hands, young parents with small children, two old women walking arm in arm, the smaller one leaning against her friend for support. He wanted permanency in his life. He really did believe Paul would be around for a long time, and Joe still couldn't believe he was gone. Shocked that he didn't see it coming, that maybe he didn't know Paul that well after all, or perhaps that he was so wrapped up in his own life that he didn't see the signs. They rarely argued, never fought. Joe rolled his shoulders. Obviously Paul was unhappy enough to leave, but to end it with just a note? That last night they had dinner, chatting about meaningless things, and yet Paul said nothing about his plans. Again in bed that night, nothing. Their difference in ages had never mattered before, Joe thought. He stopped in front of a boutique that offered body piercing and tattoos. He'd pierced an earlobe back in the '90s – the hole was closed up now - but he couldn't imagine having anything else on his body perforated. A tattoo? Maybe. Maybe something symbolic. He considered it as he stared at the window. Someone brushed against his back. He turned, but the offender had moved on.

Paul had two tattoos, a downward-pointing pink triangle on his left butt cheek and the Japanese symbol for fire on his right pec. Well, Paul told him it was the symbol for fire; Joe couldn't be sure.

He stepped inside. Clean, bright. No waiting line. He looked around at the designs. I don't even know what I'd get, he said to himself. *What am I doing here?*

"You want tattoo?" a young man approached. He was small, wiry, with a shaved head and a black goatee.

"I don't know, I was thinking about it," Joe said. His skin grew warm and moist and he removed his cap to brush a hand over his forehead.

"You pick something," the man said, waving around at the designs on the walls.

Joe took off his sunglasses and continued to look around, even as his armpits dampened. Each of the

Chinese symbols had a word beneath it. He found a symbol for water and stared at it.

"You like this one?" the man pointed. Joe could only nod. His mouth was dry and his tongue felt thick, too big. Water.

"Okay, you come back here." Joe followed the young man to a room in back. It was like he was watching a movie, and he was in it. He felt as if someone was directing all his movements.

"Where you want?" The young man washed his hands at a sink and pulled on gloves.

Oh God, where do I want it, thought Joe. And wait, who is this guy. How do I know he'll be any good. What if it comes out horrible, what if I get infected. His heart hammered in his chest and he thought he might pass out. He held up a hand and saw it was shaking.

"Hold on," he managed to croak. "Not so fast. I'm just looking right now."

The young man looked him up and down, and Joe saw himself, old, decrepit, a dinosaur. *I'm trying too hard. I have to get out of here.*

"Listen, thanks for your time. I'm going to think about it, and if I want to go ahead, I'll be back." He hurried out of the shop and into the bright sunshine. Fumbling in his pocket for his sunglasses, he put them on, darkening the bright light. What the hell am I doing, he thought. I almost got a fuckin' tattoo on...where? My ass? My shoulder? Idiot, he chastised himself silently. He regained his composure and walked purposefully to the Empress. Edamame will bring me back to reality, he told himself.

8

July 3 – 150 days to go

Kellie wished she could just walk up and ask Elizabeth about this guy Bill Hopedale. After all, it wasn't like she was a teenager. What kind of law does he practice? Is he divorced? Widowed? A bachelor? It was unlikely he'd never been married, Kellie thought. She dreaded those first-date conversations, when he'd ask her about the past twenty years of her life, like she could sum them up over cocktails, or a burger. I could just tell him I've been married twice and wait for his reaction. I could tell him my half-brother murdered our mother and see what he says about that. I could sabotage this date so easily, she told herself. Of course, Ed could have told him everything; they worked together. But Ed wouldn't, she knew that. Elizabeth, maybe, but not Ed.

There was a light knock on the door to her office, which was open. Camille's body filled the entire doorway.

"Hey, Kellie," she said, flattening her palms against her skirt.

"Hi, Camille. What can I do for you?" Kellie liked Camille. Of all the girls at the television station, Camille seemed to be the most genuine. One of those big girls with an easy laugh, but Kellie knew that the jokes and laughter were just cover. Camille was always willing to be set up for a date. Lots of first dates, never a second, though.

She took a step forward into Kellie's office. Her blouse gapped open at the space between her ample breasts, and

Kellie could see a bit of her bra. She wondered if she should offer a safety pin, or would that be offensive? She left it alone. One of the other girls would surely tell her. They'd be only too happy to tell her.

"I'm doing one of those home parties, nice kitchen stuff," Camille began, folding her arms together under her bosom. Kellie twirled her pen.

Camille giggled. "I thought about doing one of those naughty nightie parties, but you win free stuff, and it's not like I'd ever have a chance to use it, you know?" She laughed again and tugged at her skirt. "So anyway, I decided on a kitchen gadget thing. I know it's coming up on the holiday weekend, so I thought I'd do it next Tuesday. Right after work. And I'll have food and everything. If you're not busy, that is. Otherwise, I have a catalogue. But you don't have to buy anything!" She stopped and took a breath.

"Sure, let me check. But if I can't make the party, I'll get something from the catalogue," said Kellie. Maybe that would be enough, to just buy something.

"You don't have to, you know."

Kellie smiled at Camille. "I know."

Camille's neck flushed red. "Okay, thanks, but I hope you can come, too," she said before leaving.

Kellie thought about making an excuse. The last thing she wanted to do was spend an evening with her co-workers, and she assumed they'd all be women. She liked Camille enough, but the others? She imagined nothing but office gossip all evening. These news people thought they had the scoop on everything, and if they didn't, they just made things up.

She pushed back from her desk and stood. She needed to walk, take a little break. But just as she was about to exit her office, her intercom buzzed. She took a few steps back and pressed the speaker button. "Yes?"

"Kellie, would you come to my office, please?" Elizabeth's voice sliced the air.

"On my way," Kellie said, grabbing her jacket.

*

Kellie rapped on Elizabeth's open door and waited. Without looking up, Elizabeth raised her index finger. Her head was bent over a file that lay open on her desk. After a long minute, she straightened in her chair.

"Come in, Kellie," she said, moving the file to one side of her desk. She clasped her perfectly-manicured hands in front of her like a proper schoolgirl and waited until Kellie was seated opposite her.

"How are you?" she asked. Kellie knew she didn't really care.

"I'm fine, thanks." Kellie glanced out the big window at the buildings across the park. "It's warm today." She looked back at her boss. Steady, she told herself. And for probably the millionth time, she reminded herself that if Ed loves this woman, she can't be all bad.

Elizabeth smiled and ran a hand from her forehead across her hair, which was pulled back from her face and twisted into a simple knot.

"We're looking forward to seeing you this Saturday. I do hope our invitation didn't interfere with any holiday plans you may have had."

Kellie shook her head. "Not at all." As an afterthought, she smiled at her boss.

"Ed's happy to see you again, Kellie. He asks about you often, you know." Kellie noticed flecks of gold in Elizabeth's eyes. "You don't even have one question about Bill Hopedale? Aren't you curious?" The corners of her mouth turned up slightly.

Kellie shifted in her chair. She was seated beneath an air conditioning vent and the cool air tickled her neck. "Okay, what can you tell me about him?" I'll play your game, Kellie said to herself. She clasped her hands in her lap and feigned enthusiasm.

The corners of Elizabeth's mouth turned up even more and she grinned. She laid her hands on the desk, palms down, and Kellie's eyes were drawn to the huge diamond on her ring finger. When Ed had told her back in 1995 that he was about to propose to "someone very special" in Boston, she'd felt like a Wallenda on a tightrope without any sense of balance. And then Ed offered up a safety net, a job working for his "someone very special."

"Bill's widowed, not divorced. His wife died tragically two years ago. Car accident. Better not to bring it up." Elizabeth gazed down at her ring.

"No, of course not. I wouldn't," Kellie said. But she was sure Bill Hopedale knew about her mom. And besides, if they started seeing each other, they'd have to talk about things. Things neither of them wanted to talk about, like how his wife died. How her mother died.

"He has one grown daughter, living in Vermont, I think. A grandchild, or two, I don't know. I asked Ed for some information. I met Bill years ago, when he and Ed started working together. I recall meeting his wife." She stared out the window.

Kellie crossed her legs. "What does he look like?" She stared until Elizabeth turned back to face her. Yes, it matters, she thought. And Elizabeth knew it. *She just wanted me to ask. Well, I'm asking.*

"He's not ugly, Kellie! We wouldn't introduce you to someone unattractive." Kellie dug her nails into her palms so hard she was sure she'd drawn blood.

"That's not what I meant," she said.

"No, of course not," Elizabeth said, rolling a pen between her fingers as she pursed her lips. "He's probably six feet tall, balding but not bald. Fit. He's a year younger than Ed. Fifty-six. That's not too old for you, is it?"

And what if it was, Kellie thought. She didn't know why, but she wanted to smack Elizabeth across the face.

"As I said, I'm really looking forward to your party," Kellie said evenly. She looked down at her hands and unclenched them.

"Excellent. Well, enjoy the holiday," Elizabeth replied, and picked up a file. Kellie rose from the chair and walked out of the office.

*

Scott had to be careful. One of his buddies from the fire station had called to say he'd heard some guy in a bar rattling on about police and fire disability pensions.

"There's always some jerk yelling about that," Scott had said. "They never make a sound when times are good. As soon as the economy heads south, they start yapping about it. Couple of old farts in the diner were going on about it, too. But how much you wanna bet they've milked Social Security for everything they could get?"

"I'm just sayin', watch your back, brother," he'd told Scott. "You never know who people are talking to. Those undercover reporters are always looking to catch someone. Remember a few years ago when they filmed Vinny running the Boston marathon?"

"Vinny was an idiot. You don't claim asthma, get off work, and then run a friggin' marathon." Scott hung up and paced the small combination living-dining room in his apartment.

He couldn't lose his pension. Already forty-four, he had no intention of going back to work. But without the disability pension from West Alton, he'd be totally screwed. He'd banked over a hundred thousand since he first started collecting, but if they took it away, he'd have nothing else to live on. And forget moving to Florida. He'd never be able to leave.

So he kept the motorcycle in Will's shed, and it pissed him off. Couldn't even be seen riding his own fuckin' bike. Christ. No one ever bothered us before, he said to himself.

Now, just because the state is having its own financial problems, they want to screw all of us. He couldn't wait to get the hell away from this place. Down south, where the weather was always good. No blizzards, no ice. Where they'd just leave him the hell alone.

His phone rang again. He checked the caller ID. Liz. Again. He let it ring twice before finally picking up. "Hey."

"Hey yourself," she said in that flat voice that sounded like she was already bored with the conversation. "I been callin' you, baby, what the hell?"

"Busy." He dropped to the couch. "Sorry." Liz wasn't all that bad. He never had to work too hard with her, and she was usually game for anything. "How you been?"

"Alone. Horny." She laughed, a hoarse bark that came from twenty years of smoking two packs a day. She was trying to quit, but she told Scott the cigarettes helped keep her weight down. "You want company tonight?"

"It's hot as hell in this apartment, Liz. I've been sleeping on the porch." Scott pulled his tee shirt up to wipe his face. Even his head was sweating.

"So come here then. I got A/C." He heard her suck on a cigarette, but didn't say anything. Her addiction was her problem. "I'll be at Lucky's tonight either way," she added. "Maybe I'll see ya later." He heard the line go dead, just like that. Liz never said goodbye before hanging up. That was Liz, not whiny, not clingy. It didn't matter to her one way or the other. Part of him liked that about her. Another part of him wished she needed him more. Scott scratched his belly. Liz was a lot easier than most of the women he'd been with. What the hell, he thought. Getting laid in the air conditioned comfort of her basement apartment meant he could leave when he felt like it. And if he got up early enough, he could swing by Will's house, get his bike from the shed, and head to the beach. Screw them; he knew the state investigators would never be working on a holiday.

He sat in front of his computer and checked his mail. There was still the message about the reunion. No, he wouldn't bring Liz. Scott figured that after twenty-five years, there would be women who were newly-divorced and looking. At their peak, right? Divorced women in their forties were needy and desperate. As long as they weren't old, saggy, and bitter. A guy in his forties could still snag a young chick.

The sound of young female voices drew his attention to the window. Outside in the parking lot, three girls slipped papers under the windshield wipers of cars in the lot. He watched them move from car to car. One of them leaned over his car and lifted his windshield wiper. Her pink shorts had "juicy" printed across the ass. Scott stared. Nothing like advertising it, he thought. She straightened up and walked over to join the other two. All three girls wore ponytails and shorts. Miss Juicy was short and chubby, with a little roll of fat that spilled over her waistband. Muffin top, they called it. She was definitely a muffin top.

He watched as they papered the other windshields and then retreated to the apartment building across from him. He trotted down a flight of stairs to the parking lot and pulled the sheet from under his wiper.

"BLOCK PARTYYY! FRI NITE, RIGHT HERE IN OUR PKG LOT!!! BYOB – WE'LL HAVE GRILLS SET UP!! MEET UR NEIGHBORS AND CREATE SOME FIREWORKS!!!! ABBY, CHLOE, MOLLY (BLDG C)"

Scott wondered which one was Miss Juicy.

9

July 6 – 147 days to go

Kellie was at Salon Umi for the whole package: manicure, pedicure, waxing, spray tan, hair color and style. Elizabeth and Ed Ford's dinner party was that evening at their East Side home and Kellie was going to a lot of trouble for this Bill Hopedale. She tried to imagine him from the little bit of info Elizabeth had provided: older, widowed, balding. And don't ask about his wife's death. Jeez, Elizabeth, Kellie thought, like I would ever do that. He has baggage. Well, we all have baggage.

She sat in the stylist's chair and faced the mirror. At forty-three, Kellie could pass for a woman ten years younger. Her hair showed not a bit of gray, and her reconstructed face revealed only the slightest of crinkles around the eyes. She stayed out of the sun; that's what spray tans were for. Still, when she looked in the mirror, she saw teenage Kellie, with lank hair hanging limply down the sides of her acned face, a hooked nose, bad teeth. Plastic surgery may have changed her outward appearance, but it couldn't recreate the memories.

She extended her legs and wiggled her toes. They poked out from beneath the hem of the lavender drape that covered her from neck to ankles. Her toes were painted pale orange, like sherbet, as were her short fingernails, to complement the outfit she'd already chosen for that evening. All unnecessary hair had been waxed away. A lot of effort for a blind date. It didn't matter,

Kellie told herself again. Taking time to look good was all part of it. And it was Elizabeth's house, so she was still attending as an employee of Channel 8. Lifting her gaze to the mirror, she smiled at the reflection, then broadened her grin, showing perfectly straight white teeth.

"You're happy about something!" Fabio taunted in his singsong voice. He swayed his narrow hips as Shakira sang about whenever and wherever. Kellie looked up at Fabio's image. He had sharp cheekbones and blond tips on his spiky hair. His dark eyes sparkled.

"Your name's not really Fabio, is it?" She tilted her head at him and raised her just-waxed eyebrows. He bent at the waist to whisper in her ear.

"We all have secrets, don't we, darling?"

*

Scott woke up and forgot for a moment where he was. His hand crept across the bed to emptiness and he let out a sigh of relief. He lifted his head, squinted at the clock. Nearly noon. Holy shit, he thought, I must have really been wasted last night. He turned over to lie on his back and tried to piece together the events of the previous night.

The block party was in full swing when he finally ventured down to the parking lot. He'd spied on the activities from his apartment window, and waited until there were plenty of people in the area before he joined them. Pools of light illuminated the gas grills that had been rolled out around the perimeter by some of the residents. Most of the people were young, or younger. Scott figured the average age was late twenties, early thirties. A few people had set beach chairs in circles, and they clustered together. Recycle bins were filled with ice and bottles of beer. Scott carried one of those little coolers that held a six-pack, and pulled a cold can from its plastic ring. There were no kids. Scott surveyed the scene before he spotted a group of a dozen or so young women, and he sauntered over to them.

He introduced himself and was met with a giggly chorus of first names: Deb, Hannah, Lily, Brittany, two Rachels, and, of course, Abby, Chloe, and Molly. Molly. Miss Juicy. She was the round one with the white car, and she told him she was a grad student in oceanography at the university. He watched as she'd downed one bottle of hard lemonade after another. He tried to keep up, and forgot about going back to his apartment to retrieve the thick steak in his fridge. Someone offered him a hot dog, and he remembered Molly grabbing it out of his hand and using it as an X-rated prop. She never took her eyes off him. Her signals couldn't have been clearer. Then, when someone started playing hip-hop music from an old boom box, she'd backed up to him, rubbing her backside into his crotch, the most obvious of gestures.

So why hadn't she come back to his apartment with him? He tried to remember details, but couldn't. Dancing in the parking lot, yes, he recalled, his hands buried into the squishy flesh of her abdomen, keeping her pressed against him as her movements had the intended effect. He had no idea how he got back home. He pressed his palms to his temples. A scream. A crash. Pieces of the evening flitted in front of him, like scraps of paper in the wind, but he couldn't remember enough to make sense. He rolled over and went back to sleep.

*

Cherry brought Nick and Gwen to the restaurant. Bud couldn't take the weekend off, not Fourth of July, when the Cape exploded with tourists. Lots of young professionals from Boston drove down, and, unlike their parents who were loyal customers of O'Malley's or Aidan's, they chose vindaloo over shepherd's pie. The Kashmir Grille's clientele was mostly under thirty years old. Different tastes. Plenty of people told Bud an Indian restaurant would never make it on the Cape, but he'd proved them wrong.

They were greeted by Nita, Bud's assistant manager, who hugged Cherry and Nick and offered her hand to Gwen before seating them at a table at the front of the restaurant. She leaned down to whisper to Cherry as she laid menus on the table.

"You look good! Feeling okay?" Her light accent reminded Cherry of cut glass, that Indian inflection that charmed her so much the first time she'd heard Bud speak.

Cherry smiled and nodded. She didn't want to talk about any of it, not today, not this weekend. Her mastectomy was scheduled for the sixteenth, a Tuesday. Double. Total. Ta-ta to the tatas. Breastsbegone. Whatever. She would direct the conversation away from any mention of the upcoming surgery, especially with Nick at the table.

"I'm feeling great, thanks," she replied, opening the menu. After a few minutes, she glanced to the back of the restaurant, where Nita stood talking to Bud. Cherry watched Nita lift her face and stroke his upper arm. She looked back at her menu and blinked once, twice. When she looked up again, Gwen was staring at her hard.

"I'm thinking tikka masala," Cherry said, looking back at the menu. She kept her voice even, for Nick. Nick, with his back to Nita and Bud, frowned at the menu.

"Mom, you always have the same thing," he groaned. "Try something different for a change!"

She blinked again, hard, and set her jaw. "There's nothing wrong with choosing the same food," she said in a sharp voice.

Bud never paid all that much attention to her breasts, she thought. Not like the other boys. He told her she had great legs. She always wore skirts for him, and kept her necklines high. He'd told her it wouldn't matter, that he'd love her the same with breasts or without. She dared a peek to the back of the restaurant again. Bud looked up at the same time and grinned at her. He raised one finger, letting her know he'd stop by momentarily.

A waiter stood at her elbow. Cherry didn't recognize him.

"Dude!" said Nick, fist-bumping the young man.

"Hey, Nick. Hey, Mrs. Patel," he said. He looked to Gwen, unsure, then smiled and nodded.

Cherry looked at the waiter, then at her son.

"Mom, this is Kyle. From school."

"Of course. Hi, Kyle. This is Nick's aunt, Ms. Weiss," she added, waving a hand in Gwen's general direction.

Should I have remembered this boy, Cherry wondered. Maybe the cancer is in my brain, too. Maybe I'm losing my mind. Maybe I'm just seeing things and imagining circumstances that aren't true. Or not.

"Are you ready to order?" Kyle waited, a small pad nestled in one hand, a pencil in the other.

"Order for me, honey," Cherry said, getting up from the table. "I'll be right back." She hurried toward the restroom behind the bar, just as Bud walked to their table from the opposite direction.

10

July 6 – 147 days to go

Kellie arrived back home from the salon at four in the afternoon and turned up the air conditioning. A light drizzle outside wouldn't wash away the humidity. The condo was stuffy and she felt a trickle of sweat inch its way down her back. A quick shower, without getting my hair wet, she told herself.

She pulled a pitcher from the refrigerator and poured iced tea into a tall glass, then dropped into an overstuffed chair to read her mail while the room cooled down. Bills from the cable company, electric company, credit card. Two catalogues, one for expensive jewelry and one for garden supplies.

Kellie wished she didn't have to go to this party. And this guy, Bill Hopedale. I should get an Oscar for the performance I'll be putting on tonight, she thought. Smile, laugh, nod. Kellie sighed and stood up, pulling her dress away from her thighs. She wanted to nap in the dark bedroom, or maybe take a cool bath instead of a shower.

She pulled off her cotton dress and underwear, and tossed them in the hamper. At least she had a washer and dryer right in her condo, she thought, remembering all the times she'd have to do her wash at the Laundromat, the creeps in there watching her pull her bras and panties from the dryer, licking their lips and winking at her. One guy had actually offered to wash her laundry for her. She'd never gone back there again.

She rummaged through a drawer in the bathroom and found a plastic shower cap from some hotel, pulled it over her head and tucked the ends of her hair inside. She stepped into the tub and eased herself into the cool water. It was chilly, too cold really, but she only needed five minutes to wash away the sweat and lower her body temperature.

She took her time applying makeup, not too much, and wore the new summer dress she'd bought last month, before she even knew about the party. She slipped her feet into low-heeled sandals and checked herself in the mirror.

"Kellie Blunt," she said to her reflection, still seeing the girl from high school. In spite of all the work, Kellie was the same person, and no amount of outward alterations would change that. "Kellie Campbell," she said, louder. "Nice to meet you." She smiled and batted her eyelashes at the mirror.

At five minutes to six, she locked her door and stepped into the elevator. The doors opened to the lobby of her building and Kellie saw Kirby standing guard. She liked that there was a doorman in her building. Kirby opened doors, accepted deliveries, and he had a razor-sharp memory. At night, no one could just walk into the building, which gave Kellie at least a semblance of protection. When Kirby was off, Mitch took his place. Mitch was built like a fireplug, but quick on his feet and just as polite as Kirby.

"Good evening, Miss Kellie," he said. He stood well over six feet tall and must have been a linebacker in a former life; his upper arms strained the sleeves of his jacket and his shoulders were as wide as a truck. Kellie noticed that his trousers were sharply creased and pictured Kirby standing at an ironing board. He kept his hair close-cropped, like a Marine or a police officer, and sported a tiny gold hoop in his left ear.

"Hi, Kirby," said Kellie. "I need a taxi, please."

"Sure thing, miss," he said, and with one step was behind his desk. He picked up a white telephone receiver and punched in some numbers. He said only two words: "Colonnade" and "thanks." He replaced the receiver and glanced up at Kellie. "On the way."

"Thanks." Kellie shifted her weight and tried to look bored.

"Where you headed tonight, Miss Kellie?"

"Oh, just up to the East Side," she said. "It's a house party, and I can't walk there." She thought, *well, I could, but my boss won't let me.*

"Not at all, miss. Rain stopped now, but it's never a good idea for a young woman to walk alone in the city."

Kellie was sure she wasn't much younger than Kirby. They might even be the same age, but she appreciated his words. She pressed her lips together, knowing she'd have to reapply lipstick in the cab.

"They had another mugging up at Brown," Kirby said. Kellie could see the tendons in his neck, tight and ropy. That shirt must be uncomfortable, she thought, with such a thick neck. Some of his skin spilled over the collar, and she wanted to suggest he loosen that top button.

"That's just terrible," she replied, not knowing what else to say. You can't live your life afraid of everything, right?

A car with "Friendly Cab" emblazoned on its side pulled up to the entrance. Kirby walked ahead of Kellie to open the door. Outside, he opened the back door of the cab and, as Kellie slid into the seat, Kirby said to the driver, "Young lady's going to a residence up the hill." Just before he closed the door, he said, "You have a pleasant evening, Miss Kellie." And without waiting for a reply, he shut the door and strode back inside the Colonnade.

"25 Clarke Street," she said to the driver, who nodded and navigated the one-way streets up the hill to the fashionable East Side. Kellie looked out the window at stately houses and saw plenty of people walking on the sidewalks. No one seemed afraid to be outside on a muggy July evening. College was out for the summer, and most of the students went home, to places far from Rhode Island. Elizabeth and Ed Ford lived in one of those historic houses that lined the streets around the sprawling campus of Brown University. The cab slowed, then stopped in front of the house, a three-story colonial painted light gray, with a bright red door. Kellie paid the driver, who turned in his seat and handed her a business card.

"You call me for a ride home? There, that's the number. Just call. I'll pick you up and take you home." Kellie imagined him working late, waiting for the telephone to ring.

"Okay, thanks," she said. She exited the cab, taking care not to slam the door, and took a deep breath before walking up to the entrance. The front door was closed, and Kellie hoped it meant the Fords had central air conditioning. She pressed an antique brass doorbell and waited. There was no breeze, just the heavy, wet air clinging to her skin and hair.

A young woman opened the door. Kellie was startled; she craned her neck to look at the house number again.

"Is this the Ford house?" Did Ed and Elizabeth have live-in help? Did they hire this woman for a dinner party?

"Good evening," she said. Kellie heard what she guessed was a Caribbean accent. The woman was dressed in black Bermuda shorts and a crisp white shirt. Her brown legs were tight and lean and she wore black huarache sandals. Her hair was braided tight to her head and pulled back in a knot at the nape of her neck. "Please, come in." She opened the door wider and gestured for Kellie to enter. The air inside the house was much cooler and Kellie smiled with relief.

Elizabeth swept up to greet her. "Kellie!" She gave her a half-embrace, not really touching, and Kellie heard her kiss the air next to her cheek. Elizabeth looked so different. At the news station, she was straight and tailored, every hair in its perfect place. Here she looked almost liquid, in a long flowing dress, her hair loose and wavy, her bare arms tanned and toned. Elizabeth was simply stunning, and Kellie felt two separate rivulets of sweat roll down her back.

She willed her feet to not run out the front door, past the island girl in huarache sandals. Instead she said, "Elizabeth, thank you for having me. What a lovely house."

"I'll take you for a tour later," Elizabeth whispered, one hand held to the side of her mouth. "Come on, we're having drinks on the deck. I want you to meet Bill!" Elizabeth took Kellie's hand and led her through the foyer, past what looked like a library, through a massive kitchen of shiny stainless steel and black granite, where the island girl was assisting a tall, thin man in a white chef's coat. Okay, Kellie thought, so maybe these two were just hired to do the food. She followed Elizabeth out the sliding doors to the deck. Two couples were seated at a square, glass-topped patio table. There was an oversized bottle of wine and half-full glasses on the table, and tiny white lights twinkled under a green canvas umbrella. The deck was enormous. At one end, Kellie noticed two chaise lounges with a small table between them. A gleaming stainless steel grill, bigger than any grill Kellie had ever seen, was just off the deck, on a concrete slab away from the pool. The pool wasn't big, as the deck took up most of the back yard, but it was so pretty. Lights immersed in the water gave a sensuous, shimmery aura, perfect for a night swim, she thought. She had a wild vision of the classy little dinner party giving way to a drunken orgy of eight people skinny dipping in the pool and nearly laughed out loud. The yard was fenced, and tall shrubs, meticulously trimmed, provided total privacy.

"Everyone, this is Kellie Campbell, an associate producer who works with me. Kellie, I don't expect you to remember everyone's names right off." Elizabeth turned slightly and began introducing the other guests. Which one is Bill Hopedale, Kellie wondered.

"Marcia Blue and her husband Alex. Tricia Flair, Gregg Carr." Kellie looked at each one as their name was mentioned. She smiled and shook the hands that were extended to her.

"Nice to meet you," Kellie murmured. Maybe he didn't show after all, she thought. Maybe he changed his mind and didn't want this blind date any more than I did. She was about to sit down in an empty chair when Elizabeth took her hand again and led her away from the table to a bar that was set up at the opposite end of the deck. Kellie saw Ed's gesturing arms before she saw the rest of him, as he and another man walked back from the far side of the pool. She discreetly pressed her right palm against her dress and ran her tongue over her teeth inside her mouth.

"Oh, Kellie," said Ed, opening his arms to embrace her. "So good to see you again." He kissed her cheek. She scowled up at him, then broke into a grin. She knew her date was standing there watching the two of them, but she didn't care. It was Ed, after all, and she hadn't seen him since she first moved back to Rhode Island. She accepted his bear hug like a kid sister would from her older brother.

"It's good to see you, too," she said, her voice muffled against his mustard-yellow golf shirt. She inhaled his familiar scent, green and woodsy, and relaxed. Even in this humidity, his shirt was dry. As she pulled away, he put a hand on her shoulder, and turned her toward Bill.

"May I introduce my colleague, Bill Hopedale," he said, and Kellie felt everyone's eyes on her. Elizabeth probably told them all that this was a fix-up, she thought, and the tension returned to her shoulders. She raised her face to Bill.

"Hi, Kellie," he said, and when he smiled, Kellie saw the dimple in his left cheek. His thinning hair was a mix of blond and silvery gray, and it looked good on him.

"Hi, Bill," she said, oblivious to the six other people she knew were staring at her. She held out her hand, not sure if it was too formal, but he took it in both of his. His hands were warm and dry. She thought they might be sweaty, as she was sure hers were, in this humidity. She smiled, and for the first time since entering the Fords' house, she wasn't faking it.

"Kellie, what'll it be?" Ed stood ready at the bar with an expectant smile on his face.

"White wine would be great, thanks."

She looked at the glass Bill was holding. It was clear, so she guessed either vodka or gin with either tonic or soda, and a slice of lime. He had long, slender fingers, like those of a pianist, and clean, trim fingernails.

From behind the bar, Ed held up his glass. "Dark rum and tonic. With lime." He raised his eyebrows. "Nice summer drink. Try one?"

Kellie laughed. "Okay, dark rum and tonic then." She glanced again at Bill and felt something inside begin to unclench, to smooth out. No more than two of these, she warned herself silently. Stay sharp, Kellie. Don't want to get stupid now. Not with Bill Hopeful. Not in front of Elizabeth and Ed and those others, whose names she'd already forgotten.

Bill took the drink from Ed and handed it to her. "Cheers," he said, looking straight into her eyes. He tapped her glass with his and added, "Come this way for just a second." His voice was rich and creamy, and Kellie imagined he was a good singer, too. He led her away from Ed and the bar to an unlit corner of the deck, where they stood in front of the chaise lounges, away from the rest of the group. He motioned for her to sit, and when he took the chair opposite, his knees bumped hers.

"Kellie, I don't want this to be awkward. I know we're a little old to be fixed up, and I don't want you to be uncomfortable this evening."

"I have a feeling that the others are very interested in how we get along." She inclined her head toward the group at the other end of the deck.

"Yeah, but who cares? Marcia and Alex live next door; I've met them before, and Tricia works at another law firm. Look, I'd have preferred to meet you alone, one-on-one, so we could have a normal conversation, but we're here, and you're really pretty, so I just wanted to get that out of the way." He stood, towering over Kellie, and extended his hand to help her to her feet. She rose and stood next to him, and realized she could have worn higher heels. She'd remember that, in case they had another date. A real date. He's as nervous about this as I am, Kellie thought, and knowing that made her happier about the evening. It'll be fine. She smiled up at Bill Hopedale and said, "Let's go join the others."

The dinner party was better than Kellie thought it would be. They did end up eating inside, when the mosquitoes became a nuisance, in spite of all the contraptions Ed had set out around the deck. The young woman who had opened the door when Kellie arrived served the food, too. Kellie still thought it was a bit much to hire her to serve food when there were only eight people. But that was Elizabeth; she wanted everyone to know she had the means to hire a cook and server for the evening.

She looked over at Ed, who caught her eye and winked. She missed him, missed the long talks they used to have back in Chicago. But that was before. Before she ended up in the hospital, bruised and broken, and before he married Elizabeth. Everything had changed after that. Not that Ed wasn't still a friend, but Kellie knew how things were. She didn't want to get in the way, and she never wanted Elizabeth to think that the love she felt for Ed was romantic. It wasn't. It was just that Kellie owed everything to Ed; she didn't think Elizabeth could understand the depth of gratitude she felt toward him. So when he winked at her, she grinned back at him, and that had to be enough.

"I just can't keep up with it," said Marcia, and Kellie wondered what they were discussing. She hoped no one asked for her opinion on a topic she wasn't following.

"When you have teenagers, you *have* to keep up," Tricia said, rolling her eyes and laughing. "I bought my first smartphone last year, and I still don't know how to upload a picture."

As the plates were cleared from the table, everyone pulled out their cell phones. Kellie looked to Bill, who shrugged and unclipped his phone from a belt holster. Kellie's phone was in her purse, which was on a table somewhere. She didn't want to have to excuse herself to go get her phone, so she sipped ice water instead.

And then a few of them held up their phones and started taking pictures, and Kellie turned away from them. She looked to Bill, whose phone simply rested on the table, face down.

"Should I go get my phone and take photos, too?" He picked up on her sarcastic whisper, and his eyes crinkled at the corners.

"Come on, you two! Let me get a shot!" Marcia shouted, her words colliding into each other. Marcia's husband patted her arm and whispered something in her ear, to which she replied, "I am not!" She shook his hand off her arm and held her phone up.

Kellie turned her head away from Marcia and implored Bill with her eyes. "Please," she mouthed, hoping he would understand.

"Kellie and I are going for a walk. We'll be back," he said, standing up and holding out his hand. Kellie placed her hand in his and pushed back her chair as the others just stared.

"Going for a dip?" Marcia made dopey eyes at Bill as her husband took her wine glass and handed it to Elizabeth.

"Just a walk for now," Bill replied evenly. Kellie liked the feel of his hand on her back as they made their way outside, and later as he walked her to his car to give her a ride home. He opened the passenger door and Kellie slipped into the cool leather seat. The car still smelled new. She glanced into the back seat before Bill opened his door. Pristine, she thought, and let out a breath she didn't realize she'd been holding.

They said little as she directed him down the hill and through the streets of Providence to her building on Empire Street. "This is it," she said, pointing.

He stopped the car across the street from the Colonnade but left the air conditioner running. "Well, that's over," he said, exhaling. "Are you as relieved as I am?"

"It could have been worse. I had a vision of Marcia jumping into the pool."

He chuckled. "Well, we were the first to leave, so maybe she did. Listen, Kellie, I'd love to see you again. Just us next time and not six other people. Would you have dinner with me?"

Kellie had considered that question even before Bill asked. She was thinking about it during dinner, their walk, and the short ride down the hill. She knew she wanted to see him again. It had been a long time since she'd been on a date, especially a good one. Time to jump back into the pool, as it were.

"I'd love to. That would be great." She meant it, and somewhere deep in her gut she felt a flutter.

"Okay if I call you?" He looked nervous again. Apparently he didn't go on a lot of dates, either. She nodded and said, "Let me give you my number." He unclipped his phone and punched in her number as she recited it to him.

His fingers tapped lightly against the steering wheel. He didn't look at her when he spoke. "You have no idea how much I want to kiss you," he said in a barely audible voice.

Kellie's pulse quickened and the fluttering intensified. He's more nervous than I am, she thought. "I think I know," she said. Oh, did that come out sounding flippant? She squeezed her eyes shut for an instant, wishing for a do-over. But Bill inclined his head to hers and she turned to meet his lips. They kissed, and it was a good first kiss. When it was over, she wished they could do it again.

"Talk tomorrow?" She had her hand on the door handle.

"Tomorrow," he said. He grinned like a kid. Kellie stepped out of the car and crossed the street in front of him. She lifted her hand before entering her building, where Kirby stood next to the entrance, a blockade against any intruders.

*

Kellie shivered as she walked through her front door. She'd left the air conditioning on all evening and now it was frigid. She tapped the thermostat to raise the temperature and kicked off her shoes. It was eleven-thirty, and she wondered if it was too late to call Suzanne.

She pulled out her phone and typed a quick text to her best friend.

Within a minute, her home phone rang.

"I've been waiting all night for you to call me," Suzanne said.

Kellie pressed the speaker button. "If I shout, it's only because I'm getting out of these clothes. I just got home."

She heard Suzanne's voice through the speaker. "I'll wait. You go do that and I'm going to pour a glass for myself."

Kellie pulled off her clothes and dropped them on the floor, then slid into an oversized tee shirt. She shook a baby aspirin from a small white bottle in her medicine cabinet and downed it with water she scooped into her hand from the bathroom faucet.

"Is Jake around?" She fell easily into her favorite chair.

"No, he's in Groton again. He took a double shift for weekend pay. Skye's still up in Stockbridge, but she's having a blast. She might even have a job there when the camp ends."

"That's great news." Kellie sat still, the hum of joy still buzzing around inside her. She didn't want it to stop.

"But enough about us! So, Bill Hopeful! And you were out until almost midnight - this is good news, right?"

Kellie smiled at the nickname. "I guess so. I mean, yes. I hated being fixed up, especially in front of a bunch of people I'd never met, but I like him. I felt really comfortable with him."

"Was he what you expected? I mean, you know, was he okay?"

"He's attractive, and I know that's what you're asking." She laughed and lifted her bare feet to the coffee table, looking at the orange-sherbet toes. She was glad she'd had all that pampering done earlier in the day. "He was easy to talk to. There were two other couples there besides Ed and Elizabeth. I really didn't like them."

"Well, they're Ed and Elizabeth's friends, right? You don't really like Elizabeth," Suzanne said.

"No, but I love Ed, so I tolerate Elizabeth. Plus, she's my boss. I just felt like they were sizing me up in their rich, smug, little way." She laughed at how silly that sounded, but it was true. "The best times were when we were alone together, away from the rest of them. He drove me home, and we sat in his car talking. I really like him." She drew a circle on her bare thigh with her index finger.

"Typical first date conversation?"

Kellie's fingernail left a mark on her thigh; she noticed it and stopped drawing the circle. "Just small talk. I wasn't supposed to ask about his dead wife, so I didn't. And he just asked about my job. It was fine." She knew that if they started dating, there would be more difficult conversations ahead. But that was for later. Tonight, she would enjoy the memory of his kiss.

"So I assume you're going out again?"

"He said he'll call me tomorrow." Kellie glanced at a clock on the wall. "It's tomorrow, so we'll see." Don't get your hopes up, a voice in her head mocked.

"Kell, he'll call. I'm sure of it. Sounds like a nice guy."

"Yeah," Kellie said, almost to herself. She wished she could just skip ahead, past those awkward early days of adult dating, to months from now, when they would, or wouldn't be a comfortable couple.

Suzanne yawned on the other end. "Well, I'm glad everything went well. Get some sleep, my friend."

Kellie clicked off and drank the rest of the water in her glass. Bill Hopeful. She smiled, remembering the feel of his lips on hers. It was a good blind date, better than she thought it would be. He wasn't a big drinker, either gin or vodka. If they started dating, she'd be sure to have a bottle of whatever he liked to drink, plus a mixer, on hand. If.

Of course, if it didn't work out, Kellie knew it would be awkward with Elizabeth. Then she told herself to stop projecting. Bill worked with Ed, and her relationship with Ed wasn't anything like it was when she interned for him in Chicago, before everything. She and Ed were connected only by the common thread of Elizabeth now, and Kellie knew that Elizabeth could cut it at any time.

She stood and pulled the curtain aside to look out the window. After midnight and Empire Street was alive with cars and people. There was a theatre up the block and a couple of popular restaurants. Farther up the block, she saw red and blue flashing lights.

11

July 6 – 147 days to go

Joe Traversa dressed for a party he didn't want to attend. A lot of industry types would be there, which was the only reason he decided to go. He would have much rather spent the evening, the whole weekend, lounging on his deck, staring at the ocean, sipping something cold and numbing. But he'd promised the Keenes he'd show up, and he was, if nothing else, a man of his word. Tanya and Phil Keene were like parents to him. Phil, now in his eighties, had been instrumental in launching Joe's directing career, and Joe never forgot. Tanya had kept him fed during leaner times. They were two of the most decent people in Hollywood, and Joe owed them an appearance, at least. Even if he didn't want to go.

It was a perfect July evening, and as Joe pulled out of his driveway and headed east toward Mulholland Drive, the sky behind him began to morph into a sherbet-worthy stretch of pink and orange. By the time he arrived at the address and handed his keys to the valet, the sky had darkened to a purplish blue, and the first stars were just visible overhead.

The house, while not one of the most expensive in the area, was impressive. It sat high in the hills, with stunning views from everywhere inside and out. Tanya favored black and white for décor. The grounds were meticulously landscaped, and there were small lights embedded around the lawns, up the walkways, by the pool. Joe sprinted up the steps to the front door. Tanya greeted him, wearing a long silk dress the color of saffron. She was painfully thin, Joe thought, taking care not to crush her in his embrace. Her skin was leathery, from decades in the California sun, but her pale blue eyes sparkled as she offered her cheek. Joe loved that she was one of just a few older women in Hollywood who refused to have her face lifted; she called it 'tragically unnatural.'

"I have a fellow for you, Joey!" she whispered, raising her shoulders to her ears. Oh good Lord, thought Joe, as he grinned back at his hostess. He offered his arm and squared his shoulders. Give me strength, he implored silently. Tanya broke away from him as a woman called to her from across the room and Joe headed out a back door to the deck and pool.

He recognized most of the guests. They were all involved in the business of making and selling movies, and Joe had been around long enough that he'd done business with just about all of them. Except the tall man who stood facing away from him. The man turned and Joe frowned at the profile. Familiar, but he couldn't place him.

"Joey!" Phil Keene stepped up to him, looking dapper in a white double-breasted blazer. His thin white hair was combed back from his face, and he wore eyeglasses that made his eyes look enormous, like a bug's. Everyone respected Phil Keene, and Joe shook his hand with genuine warmth and affection.

"Good to see you, Joe, my boy," said Phil. "What'll it be?" He looked down at the bottle in Joe's hand. "What did you bring me?"

"Oh!" Joe held out the bottle that was still in his left hand. He'd forgotten to hand it to Tanya. "Champagne, Phil."

"Ah, that'll never go to waste. You know everyone here, son?"

Joe bent down to be closer to Phil's ear. Phil seemed smaller; perhaps he was shrinking, thought Joe. He knew the old guy was going deaf, but he didn't want to embarrass him by shouting. "Think so, Phil. Everyone but the tall guy out on the deck. Dressed in black." Joe straightened up as Phil swiveled his head.

"That's Len Troope," he said in a whisper loud enough to be heard across the room. "New York guy. Want me to introduce you, Joey? I think he's gay, too."

"No, that's okay, Phil, I'll introduce myself. Actually, I think we met once, years ago." He patted Phil on the arm and made his way out to the deck. Len Troope. Of course. Joe remembered.

A couple of years ago, Joe had met Len one night in New York at a fundraiser for Broadway Cares. Paul was shooting a film on location in Mexico and couldn't go with him, and Len was like Joe's shadow that night, making it clear that he was available.

He walked up to Len. "Len Troope," he said, holding out his hand. Len whirled around, a look of surprise on his smooth face as recognition set in.

"Joe Traversa," he said in an oily voice, taking Joe's hand in both of his. Damn, Len looks good, Joe thought. He's lost weight. His hair is longer. And he's rocking that scruffy stubble thing.

He was momentarily lost as he stared at Len. "Great to see you again," he said, as Len finally released his hand.

"I was hoping you'd be here." Len grinned, showing newly-whitened teeth.

"Are you still in New York?" Joe edged toward the bar. He needed a drink.

"I am. Still with Profile. But it's always good to come out to LA."

Of course, Joe remembered now, snapping his fingers in his mind. Len represented a few notables. He kept a half-smiled pasted on his face and looked away as Len stared.

"Joe, you look great. Last time I saw you, when was that? Few years ago." He rubbed two fingers across his stubbly chin.

Joe nodded. "Right. Must have been 2009. The Broadway Cares benefit." Shit, wasn't there a waiter or something? Joe inched closer to the bar.

"That's right," said Len. "Are you still with Steve?"

"It was Paul, and no, we're not together. Listen, what are you drinking?" If he couldn't pour alcohol into his body soon, he'd leave.

"Hey, sorry." Len touched Joe's arm. "Come on, I'll buy you a drink. At the open bar." Len laughed.

"Sure." Joe followed Len's lead. A young man with pimply brown skin stood like a soldier, waiting.

"What do you want?" Len leaned against the bar, tall and lanky. Joe raised his head and looked into the gray eyes of Len Troope, and his heart seized in on itself. Len should be Paul. Len looked delicious. And Joe had no interest in a one-night stand.

He turned to the young man behind the bar. "Bourbon rocks," he said, thinking the kid probably didn't even shave yet.

"Chardonnay," said Len next to him.

They brought their drinks to an empty table, away from the crowds of people standing near the kidney-shaped pool. The Keenes had hosted more than one party where their guests ended up naked in the pool. Joe hoped this wouldn't be one of those nights. He looked into his glass and reminded himself to take it easy with the bourbon.

"Cheers." Len raised his glass. Joe repeated, "Cheers." He took a long swallow and felt the heat course through his body.

Len paused. "I'm in town until Thursday," he began. "You know, meetings, clients. I flew out early to have some free time." He tapped his thumb lightly against his glass.

Joe wrapped his hand around the icy coldness. He wanted to finish off the bourbon, have another, and another, until everything around him was fuzzy. But he knew he couldn't do that here. He could if he were back on his deck, though. Hell, he'd made his appearance, he'd seen Phil and Tanya, he could leave anytime. He could make up an excuse; people did it all the time.

Len inched his hand closer to Joe's but didn't touch him. "I wouldn't mind a distraction, either," he said, slivers of hope playing on his face. "Have you been to Fig and Olive yet?"

Joe sat motionless and looked at the people standing by the pool. When he turned his attention back to Len, his voice was surprisingly calm. "Call me at home later," he said. "I can't stay." He let his hand rest on Len's shoulder for a little longer than necessary before walking back into the house.

*

July 12 – 141 days to go

"Why aren't you out with him tonight?" Suzanne stirred the pot. "Taste this for me," she said, handing Kellie a spoon.

Kellie dipped the spoon and blew on it before putting it in her mouth. "Perfect," she said.

"Hmm," Suzanne murmured, and kept stirring. "You'd say that no matter how it tasted."

Kellie laughed. "Okay, no more salt!" She watched Suzanne ladle creamy soup into bowls. Leek and potato, one of her specialties. Even on a hot summer night, Kellie didn't mind. The salad was crisp and the wine was chilled. They sat across from each other at the big table.

"Well? Where is he?"

It was Friday night, and Kellie had driven down to Mystic. Jake was in Groton again. Kellie wondered about that, but she wasn't going to say anything unless Suzanne asked. No, not even then. Suzanne wasn't stupid. If Jake was staying with a woman, she'd know; she didn't need Kellie to confirm it. Besides, Suzanne said he'd be back in the morning. Kellie knew she'd probably see him before she left.

"Bill has a golf thing on Nantucket this weekend. He asked me if I wanted to go, but…no." Kellie speared a cherry tomato and popped it in her mouth. She bit and savored the inner explosion.

"No, as in you didn't want to go? Or you didn't want to spend the weekend with him?"

"I just met him last weekend! He didn't ask me just so I'd spend the weekend with him. He said it would be my choice whether I wanted to share a room with him. He offered to get me my own room. I just didn't want to be 'the girlfriend,' the new girlfriend, in front of his golf buddies. And if I *didn't* share a room with him, everyone would think I was a freak." She looked up and crossed her eyes, then stuck out her tongue. "I *am* a freak, but he doesn't need to know that yet."

"Kell, stop."

Kellie gestured with her fork. "I'm fine not going to Nantucket this weekend! I like him, I do. But I've spent a total of maybe eight hours with the guy. Last weekend's party at Elizabeth's, which shouldn't even count, since we were on display the whole time, and then he took me to lunch on Wednesday. We've talked on the phone once or twice. But he asked me yesterday! I mean, it's not like I'm going to just go with such short notice."

"You don't have to explain anything to me. I get it."

"I know. I guess I'm explaining it to myself. But I am okay with it. And I'm really happy to be *here*." She had to admit that being with Suzanne, without Bill, without Jake, was preferable. What is wrong with me, Kellie wondered. Anyone else would have just gone to Nantucket, stayed the weekend with Bill, had crazy stupid sex with him, and figured the rest out later. Not Kellie, not orderly, rule-abiding, everything-in-its-own-time Kellie.

"I'm happy you're here, too. And I'm sure he understood." Suzanne's eyes were sincere.

"I shouldn't even think any more about it. Bill's a good guy. Seems that way, at least. It was only one dinner party and a lunch. But he's kind, and funny, and, I don't know, *thoughtful*. I don't think Ed would have let me meet a schmuck, anyway." She returned to Suzanne's creamy soup.

*

After the dishes were washed and dried, Kellie poured more wine for the two of them and they sat near the window, hoping to catch an absent breeze.

Suzanne's cat jumped onto the couch and planted herself against Suzanne's thigh. She absentmindedly stroked its back. "Is he a good kisser?"

"I guess," said Kellie, glancing down at the cat. She looked up. "I mean, yeah, it was good."

"That means not so good," Suzanne said, laughing. "Just kidding, Kell. So you want to spend more time with him?"

Kellie nodded. "It's the normal thing to do, isn't it?" She blinked hard in the fading light.

"To go on dates? Yeah, Kell. Date him. Go out to dinner. Walk along the river. Let him hold your hand. You get to know him, one date at a time. You know how it's done."

Suzanne is the only person who really knows me, Kellie thought. "He doesn't drink. I'm not sure why."

Suzanne shrugged. "Okay. Does it matter?" She picked up her glass of wine. "Not even beer?"

Kellie shook her head. "At the dinner party, I couldn't tell. I thought he was drinking vodka, or gin. He didn't drink wine with the rest of us at dinner. He told me at

73

lunch on Thursday that he doesn't drink and asked if I was okay with that."

"What did you say?"

"I said it didn't matter! It doesn't. I said, as long as he doesn't have a problem if I want to have a glass of wine every now and then."

"Do you think he's an alcoholic?" Suzanne finished the wine in her glass and picked up the bottle.

"I asked him. It seemed like a logical question. I asked him if he had an addiction. He said no, and then he got quiet and changed the subject."

"Well, this is how you learn stuff about the other person, right? What does he know about you?"

Kellie ran the back of her hand along the cat's fur. "What's her name again?" She looked up at Suzanne.

"Gretl."

"Right. Gretl." She petted the cat again. "He asked me about my family. I assume that Ed hadn't told him anything if he was asking. I said my mother was deceased, and I never knew my father."

"You didn't mention Adam?"

Kellie shook her head. "I couldn't, not yet. Not on a second date. Could you imagine? 'Oh, and my half-brother is in prison for matricide.'" She leaned back and cupped her head in her hands. "I'm so fucked up," she whispered. "I'm forty-three years old and afraid to date this really nice guy."

"You're not afraid to go on a date, Kellie. You're afraid of where it'll lead." Gretl jumped down and sauntered out of the room. "You're afraid that if he knows about Adam, or your marriages, that he won't like you anymore?"

"Didn't you used to have two cats?" Kellie stood up. "I need to pee," she said, walking away.

12

July 12 – 141 days to go

Scott dialed Will's number as he lounged on his deck. From this spot he had a view of the apartment complexes and the parking lot. He looked for Molly's white car, but it wasn't there. He hadn't seen her all week, not since the block party. She'd told him she was staying around for the summer.

At the far end of the parking lot, old man Fisher's house still stood, back where the woods began. Scott remembered when the house was surrounded by nothing but fields. The family that lived in the house before old man Fisher had farmed the land for generations, but the kids all moved away and the land was sold. Now this apartment complex, four squat brick buildings and a large parking lot, dominated the area and Bradley Fisher's old white house stood at the edge, the only reminder of days past. Mr. Fisher told Scott he wanted to move to Florida, said he couldn't stand the long winters anymore, and offered to sell the house to Scott. But Scott wanted to move away, too. He wondered if he could flip the house and make some money on it. He'd have to take a look inside.

"Hey," Will said when he picked up.

"What's up, bro. You around tonight?" Scott raised his bare feet to the wicker table.

"Yeah, sure. Where's Liz?" Scott could hear the television in the background. Baseball game, but the Sox weren't playing, he knew that.

"She's at some baby shower. Fourteen Acres, you know that place?"

"Never been."

"What about Ellen? She gonna let you out of the house tonight?" Scott snickered.

Will lowered his voice. "You know how it is, brother. She gives me my Friday night as long as I take her somewhere fancy on Saturday."

Scott laughed. Jeez, these women, he thought.

"We could hit The Fool. I don't wanna go to Lucky's tonight."

"You looking for little girls, Scottso?" The Fool was frequented mostly by students from the university.

"Never hurts to look, even in the summer. Your turn to drive, Willie," he added.

"Yeah yeah. I'll be by around eight. See ya." He clicked off.

Scott set the phone back in its cradle and leaned back. There was that rush again, his blood pumping harder at the thought of someone new. He had no obligations to Liz, anyway. They weren't married. Maybe he'd see Molly at The Fool, and maybe he'd be able to find out what had happened last week.

Some of these chicks liked older guys, he reasoned. He knew what they wanted: someone to spend money on them. Fair trade, he figured. As long as she delivered. He clasped his hands behind his head and drifted into a light sleep as images of Molly's chubby thighs paraded through his mind.

*

Kellie met Suzanne's inquiring gaze. "There were a few casual dates when I was in Boston. I was always getting fixed up. Someone at work had a friend. Or a friend of a friend. They never considered whether we had anything in common. It was just, 'I know this guy, he's single.' As if that was enough. It was never enough," she said, looking at her hands. "And I hated that second date, you know where you have to talk about stuff? Because they always thought they had to do that to get to the third date, which was supposed to be the sex date." Kellie shook her head. "I hope you don't ever have to go through it." As soon as the words were out of her mouth, she wished she could grab them back. When Kellie finally looked up, Suzanne was staring across the room at nothing.

"Yeah, hope not," she whispered.

"You won't," said Kellie. "I didn't mean anything by that."

"Well, if he dies," said Suzanne. "He's very stressed out, you know, and working way too much."

"You're right. It would be great if you guys could get away for a week or two. He's got to have some vacation time coming, right?" Okay, Kellie thought, so she doesn't want to talk about the fact that Jake's been spending nearly every weekend in Groton. Really, did she believe there was that much overtime at the shipyard? With all these cutbacks?

"Maybe in September. I'd love to go to Maine in September. Remember that time when we were kids and you came with us to Freeport?"

Kellie smiled at the memory, one of a few really fond remembrances from her teenage years.

"It was the summer before senior year. I remember thinking my mother would never let me go, but she did. She even gave me ten dollars, which was nothing, but it was a lot for her. And oh, I was so happy to get away from Adam. He was such a pain in the neck then." She closed her eyes and could see her mother, in one of those long, shapeless dresses with no waist, in a faded cotton print, reaching up to pull down what Kellie always thought was a can of coffee. She peeled the lid and stuck her small hand in the can, and handed a ten-dollar bill to Kellie.

"He *was* a pest! We had fun up there. Remember the cabin? Telling ghost stories in the bed?" Suzanne shook her head.

"I remember the ocean being so cold, even in August."

"But we didn't care, Kell! We ran in anyway, even though it was freezing," Suzanne murmured. "Man, I'd never do that now. Give me a hot tub any day."

"I remember your parents being so generous and kind," Kellie said. "And corn on the cob with butter dripping down our chins. A blueberry pie from the farm stand down the road. Staying up so late giggling your dad got mad at us. That was after the ghost stories, of course." She loved that week in Maine with Suzanne's family. And she remembered how much she hated going back home after that week, and how guilty she felt for feeling that way.

"Remember that album your mom always played? Every time I went to your house…"

"Our *trailer*," Kellie interjected.

Suzanne cocked her head and smiled. "Your *home*," she said. "That James Taylor album, remember?"

Of course Kellie remembered. She could sing that album from beginning to end, every word of it. Especially that one song.

"Yeah, she loved James Taylor. And the guy from Three Dog Night. But especially James Taylor. We had this old stereo. She'd picked it up at the Salvation Army store for a couple of bucks, but it worked." Kellie pictured her mother, setting the vinyl record on the old record player, lowering the arm to the outside edge of the shiny black disc. They would stand and wait. As soon as the music started, Barbara Campbell went to another place in her mind. She was somewhere Kellie couldn't comprehend, not then, not as a kid. She was intimately familiar with that place now, though. Her mother owned maybe three or four other record albums, but that was the only one she ever played, it seemed.

"Sorry, Kell, did I make you sad?"

Kellie upended her wine glass, drinking down what was left. *Everything makes me sad*, she wanted to say. "No, it's okay, just memories." And now that song would be playing in her head all night.

Suzanne cleared her throat. "Listen to this," she said, leaning forward. "I got an email from Joe Traversa. He booked a flight to Providence for November. Said he'd go to the reunion if I'd go with him. I can't believe he's coming back here." She pulled at her short hair. She tried to twirl it around her fingers but there wasn't enough of it. "I'd so love it if you'd come with us."

Kellie's laugh filled the room. "Now I know you're drunk!" She picked up a pillow and ran a finger along the top-stitching. It looked handmade, and Kellie wondered if Suzanne had taken up sewing at some point. "Joey Traversa. He'll be welcomed back like the prodigal son. Are his parents still around?"

"They live in Florida. He's flying up from Miami, the day after Thanksgiving. I think they're both still alive. Did you ever meet his father?" Suzanne inhaled sharply. "He scared the hell out of me."

"Why?"

"He was just scary. I think he was an ex-Marine. He ran the gas station in town, and Joey said he always yelled. I mean, yelled instead of speaking normally. He yelled everything. 'PASS THE SALT!'" Suzanne tried to imitate Joe's father but collapsed in giggles.

"That must have been enjoyable," Kellie said.

"Well, plus he had a gay son. That didn't go over well."

"Did his parents know then? I mean, we kind of figured it out, but Joey wasn't all about being gay. I mean, it wasn't like he carried a banner."

Suzanne arched her back and pressed her shoulders into the sofa. Her eyes looked past Kellie when she spoke.

"He said his mother knew, but I don't know about his father. I remember Joe telling me, the day before he drove west, that it broke his heart to leave his mother alone with that man. But he couldn't live another day under his roof. So maybe his dad did know."

"Wow. Imagine, eighteen and just driving out to California. I wish I'd had that kind of courage."

"What are you talking about? You left, too, don't forget. Chicago is a long way from here."

"I had a scholarship. I couldn't turn that down. And Mrs. Walsh was the one who took care of everything, got me my dorm room, helped me with the paperwork. My mom couldn't do it, and I couldn't ask her, she'd cry every time the subject of college came up. I know it hurt her for me to leave, but she let me go. She was selfless." Kellie took a deep breath. "But Mrs. Walsh was a really great guidance counselor. I wonder where she is now." Maybe she should try and look her up, but Kellie knew she never would. Too many questions, too much to explain.

"I was mad when you left. Not mad at you, even though I thought I was mad at you for leaving. I was mad that I wasn't going with you. Joey was on the other side of the country, and you were going to Chicago. My two best friends had abandoned me."

"Oh, Suzie. But you were already with Jake," Kellie said softly. She glanced up to see Suzanne's mouth twist in a cartoonish smile.

"Yep, me and Jake," she echoed.

*

Scott and Will walked into The Fool and surveyed the scene.

"You looking for someone in particular?" Will scanned the groups of young people and buried his left hand in the pocket of his jeans.

"Met a girl last weekend at the block party. I kind of blacked out and can't remember if anything happened. I figure if she comes in here, I might be able to find out."

Will laughed and leaned on the corner of the bar. "Brother, be careful. If you banged this girl and can't remember, she's gonna hate you for not calling her. And if you *didn't* bang her, and you want to, you better spend some money on her."

Scott took a long look around. "All I know is her first name. Molly. I don't even know what apartment she lives in."

Will grabbed two bottles of beer and followed Scott to a table, along the wall where they could watch everyone in the bar. He gave his friend an appraising look. "The man in black," he commented, referring to the clothes Scott was wearing. "Old man in black," he added, chuckling.

Scott knew he needed to lose a few pounds, especially with this reunion coming up. He sucked in his gut as a trio of girls strolled by. At least he still had his hair, and it was thick, even if there were a few bits of gray here and there. Girls didn't mind that, right? What was the word? Distinguished. Yeah, I'm distinguished, he thought.

"So Liz is away, and you're chasing twenty-year-old tail."

"I'm not married to Liz. We have an understanding. Man was not meant to live with just one woman," Scott said. He'd done a couple of shots before Will had picked him up, and he was feeling good. He wanted Molly to walk through the door, and tried to make it happen with his mind. He knew people could do things like that.

"Hey, Ellen and me, we been together for almost twenty years now," Will said.

Scott turned to look at him. "Yeah, and how many chicks you banged during those twenty years, huh?"

Will laughed. "Yeah, yeah, we have an 'understanding,' too. I pay the bills, she don't ask questions."

"Well, let's get you hooked up, too, bro!" They high-fived each other. Scott kept an eye on the door. The place was filling up, mostly with twenty-somethings. Scott tightened his abdominal muscles. If Molly showed up, he'd be cool. A fat girl like that should be grateful he was interested. Although she seemed to have plenty of friends, males included, that night at the block party. The way she'd eaten that hot dog, he wasn't surprised. Party girl. Everyone's friend, with benefits. He knew the type.

Scott heard a commotion at the door as a group rolled in. Three girls and two guys. He watched them saunter in. A tall, dark-skinned girl, maybe Indian. A skinny girl with straight brown hair who looked pissed off about something. And there behind her, there she was. Juicy Molly. She had her hair pulled into two ponytails, like a little kid, and she wore a white tank top, tight, that accentuated every roll of fat. Bright pink bra straps blazed like hot slashes on her shoulders. She turned her back and Scott's eyes went directly to her plump backside. Her pink shorts had the word 'sweet' printed on the ass. What the hell, thought Scott, as he stared. First 'juicy,' now 'sweet.' This girl wanted it bad. Well, tonight you're mine, he told himself. The two guys who walked in with the girls looked gay.

"Hey." Scott elbowed Will. "The blonde in the wifebeater. That's the one from the party."

"Jesus, bro, she looks about twelve. And she could use a salad." The girls stood near the bar, while one of the boys ordered drinks from the bartender. Soon Molly was holding a bottle of Amstel Light in her chubby hand. Scott nodded with approval. Stick with the light beer, darlin'. He'd help her work off some of those calories.

Will lifted his chin as he set down his beer bottle. "You can have the fat girl. I'd go for that black chick," he said.

"She's not black," Scott said. "Indian, maybe," he added.

"The kind with the dot?" He poked his forehead. "Like a Muslim?"

"She's not black, idiot. I'll be back." Scott stood and sucked in his gut again. He made his way to the crowded bar, and as he approached the group, he made sure to squeeze behind Molly. The front of his black pants brushed against her rear. She turned and tilted her face back to look up at Scott.

"Hey, it's my neighbor!" She was drunk already, he could tell. She threw her arms around him, trying to reach his neck, and Scott felt her soft body against his. "Last time I saw you, you passed out in your apartment," she whined.

"From the party last week, yeah," he said as she pulled back. "Molly, right?" Okay, so apparently nothing had happened between them. Whew, he thought.

She grinned at him, all teeth and gums. Shiny pink gums. He reached out and grasped one of her ponytails.

"Nice hairdo," he said softly, leaning down to her face. "I'd love to buy you and your girlfriends a drink or two. My buddy and I are at a table in the back." He tugged on the ponytail and brought her face closer. Her wet blue eyes widened. "Come back to me, Molly," he whispered.

He released her ponytail and felt her breath on his face as she exhaled. "Okay," she said with a nervous giggle. Her pug nose had a tiny diamond stud in one nostril. She smelled like cotton candy and beer.

"Unless you're with one of these guys? And bring your friend." He used his chin to point to the Indian girl, ignoring the other one who still hadn't cracked a smile. She doesn't deserve a drink, Scott thought. "My buddy wants to buy her a drink, too. Please say yes."

"The boys are actually together," she said, giggling and nodding to the boys. "Maya, come here," she shouted to her friend, who stood not even a foot away. The dark-skinned girl drifted over and looked Scott up and down. "He wants to buy us drinks." She whispered something in

Maya's ear and Maya smiled. She had full lips and heavy eyebrows that Scott imagined would join together above her eyes if she didn't have them waxed.

"We'll be over," Molly said to him, tucking her thumb beneath her pink bra strap. He watched as she played with it, her eyes never leaving his. She giggled again and slipped her arm around Maya's waist. Scott gave her ponytail another tug, harder this time, then walked back to his table.

"Dude." Will lifted his hands in question.

"They're coming." Scott downed the beer in his bottle and raised a hand to signal a waitress. A woman who reminded him of Liz, hard and scratchy, stood next to him, her eyebrows raised.

"Couple more beers here, sweetheart, and don't be a stranger." He held up a folded ten-dollar bill. "That's for being efficient and friendly." She moved to pluck the bill, but he kept a firm grasp of it and wouldn't let her have it. "Couple more beers, please."

"Right away." She scurried off to the bar. Scott watched her go and puffed out his chest.

The waitress returned just as Molly and Maya glided up to their table. The men stood and pulled out chairs for the girls, who looked at each other and laughed.

Scott turned as the waitress placed two bottles of beer on the table. He handed her the ten.

"Another round? Girls, what'll it be? Shots all around?"

He made a circular motion with the index finger to the waitress, whose face showed no reaction to the scene in front of her.

Scott leaned into Molly and his lips brushed her ear. "I want to do shots with you," he whispered.

She sat back and looked at him, her eyes dewy and unfocused.

"Bring us four shots of…" he trailed off. *What do these chicks drink?*

Molly looked at Maya and laughed. "Blow Jobs! Right, Maya?" Maya rolled her eyes and laughed, showing a glimpse of dazzling teeth before her hand flew to cover her mouth.

Will stared at Maya. "I'll take a Blow Job, sure," he said.

"Excuse me for asking, but what's in a Blow Job?" Scott looked at the waitress, whose thin lips were pressed together on her narrow face.

"Bailey's, Amaretto, whipped cream, right?" Molly looked at the waitress, who nodded and headed back to the bar.

Scott glanced at Will, who gave the tiniest nod to his friend. They were in.

*

"How old are you, anyway?" Maya looked at Will first, then Scott. Her eyes were steady and hard, Scott thought. He didn't think she'd be worth the trouble.

"Just turned forty," said Will, shaving a couple of years off each of their true ages. "Trying to recapture our youth. I couldn't take my eyes off you when you walked in. Are you Indian?" Scott knew he should have made a bet with Will about this girl. He knew he was right.

Maya nodded. "But I was born in Connecticut," she said.

Molly turned her face to Scott. "What do you do?" She grasped the beer bottle's neck and ran her thumb up and down the sweaty glass.

"I'm a firefighter," he said, ignoring Will, who cleared his throat softly.

"Really?" Molly's eyes grew wide and she edged closer to him. "Wow."

"Yeah, tell us about the time you rescued a family from a burning house, bro." Will leaned forward, resting his forearms on the table.

Scott glared at his friend. "I hurt my back on the job, so actually, I'm out on disability. But they pay me," he added when he saw her face. Fuckin' Will, he thought.

"You look okay to me," said Maya.

"You a doctor?" Scott thrust his chin at her. Bitch. "You seen my MRIs, my chart?" He stared at her hard until she looked down.

"Sorry," she muttered. She looked up. "Really, sorry."

He stared at her, then turned to Will. "Anything you wanna share with the table, *bro*?"

Will gave Scott a sheepish grin. "How about I pick up the next round?"

Molly had finished her beer. Scott raised four fingers until the waitress saw him and nodded. Both girls had their cell phones on the table. Can they do anything without those stupid phones? Just like Tara when she came to visit, always with the phone. Molly picked hers up and stared at the screen, then set it back down. It was hot pink. Maya's had a leopard-print cover.

Scott leaned in close to Molly and whispered, "You're the sexiest girl in here, you know." She cut her eyes at Maya, who was deep in conversation with Will.

"Want another Blow Job?" She giggled.

Scott traced his finger along her jawline and felt her shiver under his touch. He traced down her neck, down her arm, all the way to her hand and back up again.

"You're making me wish I was back in college," he growled.

"I don't like college boys," she slurred back. "Too young for me."

The room was dark now, loud with pulsating music, and smelled of stale beer. Molly climbed onto Scott's lap and faced him. She shifted her weight back and forth and closed her eyes. Maya and Will were up dancing to whatever shit hip-hop music was playing. Scott watched as Maya stuck her bum out and pushed against Will's crotch.

Molly wrapped her arms around his neck like a fire hose. Her weight on his thighs grew heavy.

"You giving me a lap dance, Molly?" Scott dipped his finger in the remains of whipped cream from one of the shot glasses and rubbed it across her lips. She licked at it, her fat pink tongue slithering around in a circle. Her eyes were half-closed now, and Scott thought she might pass out.

"Baby, let's get outta here," he said into her ear.

"Kayyyyyy," she drawled back. She made lame gyrations in his lap and her head bobbed forward.

Will and Maya returned to the table. "I gotta go pee," Maya said. She looked at Molly and narrowed her eyes at Scott. "Moll, come with me." Molly tried to get off Scott's lap but couldn't lift herself up. Scott placed his big hands under her arms, feeling the moist pits, and lifted her off. She was unsteady on her feet but said, "Be right back. Don't go anywhere." Scott pointed to his groin and said, "You think I can walk now?"

She twisted her face into a smile and bent down to whisper to him, steadying herself with a hand on his shoulder. "I'm gonna take good care of you." The way she was slurring, Scott knew she'd be an easy score, if she didn't pass out. Maya held her arm as the girls wobbled toward the ladies' room at the far end of the bar.

Will spoke first. "Holy crap, I wanna do that girl. At first she was kinda icy, you know, but she's into me. They live in the building right across from you. I can drive, I'll take us all back."

Scott checked his watch. "What about Ellen, bro? You gotta go home to your wife."

"You my moral compass now? That girl is so hot," he whined.

"Just sayin', brother. Ellen will know. They always know."

Will slammed a fist on the table.

13

July 31 – 122 days to go

Summer progressed in Falmouth, as it did everywhere else. Cherry welcomed the breezes that drifted in from Buzzards Bay and Nantucket Sound, but the traffic was as bad as ever. More and more tourists every year added to the increased number of year-round residents and retirees. The Kashmir Grille was full nearly every night, and Bud hired extra staff for weekend catering events. Nick was learning the restaurant business from his dad, and enjoying it. Cherry had had surgery three weeks earlier and began chemotherapy treatments as soon as she was able. Her sister Gwen stayed on at the house, and Cherry told her she'd never let her leave. Whenever she had the energy, Cherry worked on the reunion.

"Gwen! Come here, I have an idea!"

Gwen appeared in the doorway, her face pink. She balanced a plastic laundry basket on her hip. It was piled high with clean clothes.

"What is it?" She set the basket on the floor, sat cross-legged next to it, and began folding towels and underwear.

"I'm going to ask each attendee to send in their most memorable event from senior year. Then I'll pick a few of the best and read them during the reunion dinner. Maybe have the others guess to see if they know who wrote it."

"That's something," Gwen murmured, focusing on tee shirts and briefs. Lots of white cotton in the summertime, all bleached and tumbled. Gwen did a load of laundry every morning, just to stay on top of it all. Thank goodness Bud had a service for all the restaurant linens.

"You don't like it?" Cherry touched her head. Her once-lustrous hair was gone, and she covered her baldness with a silk scarf. The traditional Indian *dupatta*, a very long silk scarf, served as a head covering, or *hijab*, and Cherry knew she looked more like a traditional Indian woman than a Jewish-American middle-aged woman with cancer. Bud was shocked the first time he saw her with her head wrapped in red silk.

"No, it's a good idea, sis. And something to focus on."

"Something other than Bud and Nita, you mean." Cherry leveled her gaze at Gwen until their eyes locked. "I know you think he's having an affair with her, Gwen. I just don't believe it."

Gwen bowed her head to the laundry basket. "I didn't believe it in my own marriage either, until Ned woke up one day and said he wanted a divorce. Just like that, just like adding sugar to his coffee. I know I shouldn't have been surprised; Ned went to the gym every morning." She looked up. "Just like Bud does."

Cherry snorted. "Just because Bud goes to the gym doesn't mean he's having an affair," she said.

Gwen just shook her head, and Cherry watched her auburn curls jiggle and gyrate. She tugged at the *dupatta*. When she spoke, her voice was just a whisper.

"I have no breasts. No hair. And there's poison in my body. He could leave me for all of that. But he's still here, Gwen. He's still here." She caught her breath and choked back a sob. "I'm sorry your marriage is over, but it doesn't mean mine is." She held her head up as she left Gwen to sort out the freshly-laundered clothes.

*

August 2 – 120 days to go

West Alton didn't have a country club, or even a large restaurant with banquet facilities, so Cherry had contacted the events manager at the Officers' Club in Quonset. The navy base had stood in Quonset for years. It was gone now, but the "O" Club remained, and was a popular venue for weddings. She and Gwen drove up to meet with the events manager, who had assured Cherry the date was open for their reunion.

Karen Humble walked toward them with one tanned arm outstretched. "Welcome to the O Club!" Karen reminded Cherry of a beauty pageant contestant. She took practiced steps and smiled big, real big. Her hair was blonde and fluffy and lacquered, and she showed a lot of white teeth when she smiled. There was a bit of bright red lipstick on her big front tooth, like a speck of fresh blood. And Cherry wasn't about to tell her.

"So, which of you is Cherry?" Karen pronounced it "Cheery." Cherry laid her right hand over her heart, like she was about to pledge allegiance.

"I'm Cherry," she said in a tired voice. She was exhausted already and they'd just walked into the place. She took a deep breath and steadied herself. "Could we see the room, please?"

Gwen took Cherry's arm to keep her from advancing. "I wonder if you might have a wheelchair for my sister." Cherry started to protest and Gwen raised a hand. "Don't even start, Cher." Gwen looked at Karen, whose eyes widened suddenly. She fluttered her hands and patted her hair.

"Let me see what I can do," she said and pulled out her phone. She pressed one button and waited. "Ricky? I'm in the main lobby. Would you bring a wheelchair out here right away? Thanks, doll." She pasted a big pageant smile on her face and said, "One minute. Why don't we all sit here?" She gestured to an oversized sofa in front of a fireplace.

"Thanks," muttered Cherry, as she fingered the green silk wrapped around her head. She sank into the soft cushions of the sofa and closed her eyes. Too soon, a young man appeared. This must be the very efficient Ricky, she thought. His black hair was pulled back in a neat ponytail, and he wore a dark shirt and well-fitting pants. He stood to the side of an empty wheelchair and gave an encouraging smile to Cherry.

"Thank you, doll," Karen twittered. Cherry thought she probably flirted with every man she came in contact with; perhaps it was just a part of who she was. As Ricky exited the room, Karen tilted her head at Cherry. "Shall we check out your reunion venue?" Another huge smile. Karen was really trying, and Cherry always appreciated someone who tried to be helpful and polite. Let it go, she told herself. Accept help when it's offered. She smiled at Karen, and allowed Gwen to help her into the chair.

"Super! Off we go then." Karen led the way down a long hallway, her high heels clicking along like a metronome. Gwen pushed the chair and let one hand rest on Cherry's shoulder. Cherry crossed her arm over her flat chest to lay her hand on Gwen's.

*

August 3 – 119 days to go

Kellie had met Bill exactly four weeks ago. They'd been to lunch twice since Ed and Elizabeth's party, but Bill had a case that took him to Philadelphia for the last two weeks of July. He'd called her and asked to see her tonight, and suggested a new Tex-Mex place in the city.

"I've been so busy with work, but we should try to get out on the boat one of these days, if you'd like," he said over the phone. "I could pick you up in the morning." She liked that about him; he didn't just assume that he'd be staying over with her, although tonight would be their third (or fourth) date, depending on whether the Fords' party counted. Maybe he did expect it. Either way, she agreed to the boat day on Sunday and said she'd see him in a couple of hours.

Their first lunch was at that new bistro next to the courthouse for fish tacos. It seemed as if everyone in that place knew Bill, and they hardly had any time to themselves, except for when she asked him if he had an addiction and he'd said no. The next time they had lunch, Bill told her he had to go to Philly, and that's what they talked about for an hour – Philadelphia. Kellie liked Bill a lot, and she wanted to spend more time with him, but she also wanted to know more about him. Like how his wife died, and why he didn't drink. He did talk about his daughter, who lived in Vermont with her husband, who ran a dairy farm. His two grandkids.

She looked at the clock on the wall, then turned to her bed and stripped off the sheets.

*

"Well, where do you want to go then?" Scott asked Liz when she called him.

"There's a Tex-Mex place in the city."

"You wanna go all the way to Providence?" Scott watched a silver car pull into the parking lot and wondered where Molly was.

"Come on, baby, it's not New York. They have that fire thing on the river. Pick me up on your bike." She growled into the phone like a wild tiger.

"I don't know. I gotta be careful taking the bike out. I'm disabled, you know," he added with a hard laugh.

"Then let me drive," she said, challenging him.

He exhaled loudly. "I'll pick you up at seven, in my *car*. Wear something hot."

"I always do," she replied, and clicked off.

Scott finished his beer and stared at the empty spot where Molly's white car was usually parked. He hadn't seen her since the night they'd hooked up. Since she'd run screaming from his apartment in the middle of the night. Friggin' chicks. She was the one who came on to him, talked about doing everything. Everything meant everything. All he was doing was giving her what she wanted, what she'd been advertising. They're all the same, he thought. Even fuckin' Liz. All the same.

*

Bill and Kellie were seated at a table by the window of Poblano's. The activity on Thayer Street was mesmerizing and Kellie found her eyes drawn away from Bill's too often. She forced herself to focus. Tonight was important.

When the waiter took their drink order, Bill asked for club soda and Kellie seized the opportunity.

"Will you tell me why you don't drink?" She touched his hand to soften the query. He turned his hand over, wrapping his fingers around hers.

"Yes, I'll tell you. I used to drink, not to excess, at least not very often. I'm not an alcoholic, Kellie."

"I know, you've told me that."

He pressed his lips together. "My wife drank, usually more than I did. She could hold her liquor pretty well, and her liquor of choice was scotch." He was silent for a moment, and Kellie waited. "We'd been having problems in our marriage, as everyone does, I guess. Just not connecting. We both worked a lot, and after Donna married and moved away, we just didn't enjoy each other's company that much. She – Abbie – she didn't like being on the ocean, and she had no interest in learning golf, the two things I enjoyed most. And I didn't want to go to the mall every weekend. We started spending more and more time away from each other, and when we *were* together, we argued. Especially when we drank."

He stopped talking as the drinks were set on the table.

"Give us a few minutes, please," Kellie said to the waiter. When he had retreated, Bill resumed speaking. The muscles in his face were tight and rigid.

"On New Year's night, we had a big blow-out. Bad. A lot of screaming. Words that couples should never throw at each other. We'd gone to a party two houses away and we'd both had way too much to drink, at the party and then again at home." He palmed his forehead, pushing his hair back from his forehead. "I said something particularly nasty, she grabbed the keys and stormed out of the house." He glanced up at Kellie and she saw miles of pain in his eyes.

His voice became distant, almost robotic. "A couple of miles away from our house, she wrapped her car around a tree and died instantly. Her blood alcohol level was point-two-six. No skid marks." He glanced out the window of the restaurant, at the people walking by on the street. "She didn't have her purse with her, so it took a while to trace the car's license plate. Of course, I was passed out and didn't hear the doorbell." His chin dropped to his neck.

"I'm so sorry, Bill." Kellie fumbled for the right words and realized there were none. There was nothing to say that would change any of that story.

He raised his head and ran a thumb under one eye. "Yeah. Sorry, Kellie, I knew we'd have this conversation eventually. Doesn't make it any easier."

"No, of course not," she said, and prayed he wouldn't ask her anything about her past. Not tonight. Not after this. He patted her hand.

"I'll be right back," he said, standing up and walking to the men's room.

Scott and Liz were seated a few tables away from where Kellie sat alone, waiting for Bill to return. She heard a gruff voice and looked up, and her heart seemed to freeze in her chest. Scott Hunter. Twenty-five years later, but she recognized his face. And that voice. He gestured to his companion with a beer bottle in his hand and Kellie stiffened. She looked for Bill. Where is he? She swallowed down a thickness in her throat and chanced to look at him again. He won't know me; he won't recognize this face. She turned her head, to the people passing by on the sidewalk. There were tables set up and two old women sat down right outside the window. One looked up and caught her eye. She smiled at Kellie, and, seeing no response, cast her eyes down and focused on her companion. Where the hell is Bill, Kellie thought, just as he walked back to their table.

"I'm sorry, Kellie. We should order," he said as he seated himself. He glanced up at her. "Kellie! Are you alright? You look as if you've seen a ghost."

Kellie pushed her chair back, but didn't stand. Her hands gripped the edges of the table. "I need to use the ladies' room now, Bill. Go ahead and order for both of us." She practically ran to the back of the restaurant.

She burst into the ladies' room, afraid she'd throw up, even though there was nothing in her stomach but a little dark rum and tonic. Oh God, she thought, it's him. She knew that by returning to Rhode Island, it was possible she'd see him if he was still here. Of course he's still here. Where else would Scott Hunter be? She steadied herself on the rim of the sink and took a deep breath through her mouth, letting it out as slowly as she could manage, through her nose. He'd never recognize me, she thought. I don't look anything like Kellie Blunt from high school. But the memory of him, like the toxic black water of a tsunami, threatened to pull her under and drown her. She needed to get back to Bill. Maybe they could switch seats so she didn't have to look at him, didn't have to hear that voice. She stared at herself in the mirror and slapped herself in the face, hard. It stopped the panic. She washed her hands, opened the door, and walked right into Scott Hunter.

14

August 4 – 118 days to go

Cherry wanted to work on the mass mailing. She had sent her "save the date" emails back at the end of June, and the email invitations were sent in mid-July. Now that she had mailing addresses for most of the students, a follow-up hard copy would go out. Gwen had helped her create a collage of items from 1988 for the front: a photograph of President Reagan, and underneath it, smaller photos of Bush the father and Dukakis; the Olympics logo for Calgary and Seoul (Cherry wanted to put a picture of Brian Boitano up but Gwen nixed it); a picture of *The Last Emperor* movie (Cherry insisted on that one, even though it was released in 1987, because Dr. Sing reminded her so much of John Lone); a 24-cent postage stamp, and pictures of George Michael, Michael Jackson, and Gloria Estefan. Cherry loved the invitations. The room at the Quonset "O" Club was reserved, and she included information about nearby hotels and special rates, knowing that a lot of her high school classmates would be traveling in from other states. She worked out a terrific buffet with Karen Humble and the club's chef, making sure she included vegetarian and gluten-free dishes. From the responses to her 'save the date' email, she estimated around seventy guests would be attending, including some spouses and partners. Karen had told her the room could hold up to a hundred and fifty. And Ricky from the "O" Club was very helpful in putting together a kind of computer slide show, using scanned photos from the yearbook and a few extras Cherry was able to dig up. The slide show would play throughout the evening on a big screen at the back of the room.

Bud accompanied her on all important doctor appointments, always leaving the restaurant to be by her side. Cherry never once asked him about Nita, and when Bud talked about the restaurant, he never mentioned her. If she died, perhaps Bud would marry her. Nick seemed to like Nita, and she was young, and pretty. Maybe she'd even give Nick a brother or sister. Cherry shook her head to chase the thoughts away. Bud was a good husband, supportive and helpful. He assisted with the drains, and measured the fluid output. He bathed her. He brought her fresh flowers.

Dr. Sing suggested a delay for reconstructive surgery, four to five months, until her body had healed. If she had the surgery before the reunion, she likely wouldn't be able to attend, so she told the doctor to schedule it for December. She'd manage, somehow.

"Nick-Nack, help me stuff these envelopes, honey." Nick stopped in the entryway to the dining room where Cherry and Gwen sat at the table. Gwen affixed return address labels to the envelopes. Cherry had address labels for the recipients in front of her. It would help a lot to have Nick slip the folded invites into the envelopes.

"Mom, I'm supposed to be at the restaurant early today," he said. Nick leaned his long frame against the doorway and crossed his arms over his chest. His black eyes, fringed with thick lashes, glistened like wet coal. My grown boy, thought Cherry, and grinned at him, even as her heart filled to overflowing with pain.

"Go then, get out of here," she said with a wave of her hand. He turned toward the door, but stopped. Cherry peeked up and saw him turn back and come to her. He leaned down to kiss the cheek she'd already turned up to him. "Go."

Nick let out a barely audible sigh, pulled out a chair, and began stuffing the empty envelopes. He smirked at his aunt Gwen and said, "She always gets her way, you know." He cast a sidelong glance at his mother, who beamed as she pressed address labels in the center of each envelope.

"Don't I know it, Nick," said Gwen, and patted her sister's shoulder.

Nick stopped for a moment to look at the invitations. "These are pretty cool," he said, opening one up to read what was written inside. He raised his eyebrows and nodded.

"What, honey?"

Nick bobbed his head. "I like that. Asking people to send in what they remember about their senior year. But it's been twenty-five years, Mom. You think your friends will still remember?"

"Ha ha, very funny. Of course they will!" Cherry laughed at the idea. "We're not ancient, you know."

"So, what do *you* remember most about your senior year in high school?" Nick looked at his mother as he continued to fill the envelopes.

Cherry stopped what she was doing and laid her hands on the table. She let her eyes drift around the room until she focused on a far corner, and in her mind's eye, she watched a movie of her senior year. "I was a cheerleader, and our football team won that big game against Central. No one thought we could beat them, but we did. I was going with Will Blake then. He was the quarterback. And very cute." She smiled at Nick.

"I remember him," interrupted Gwen. "He was just okay." She cast a glance at Nick and added, "Your dad is much better looking."

Cherry frowned. "He was gorgeous, Gwen." She looked down, and pressed another label on an envelope. "Although I agree, daddy is cuter." She winked at her son.

"But you broke up. Obviously. So what happened?" Nick held an invitation just above an envelope, letting it hover while he waited for his mother to answer.

"His parents didn't like me. Well, his father didn't like my father. His parents weren't going to let their Baptist son get serious with a Jew."

Nick dropped the invitation and envelope. His mouth dropped open. "Whoa. Are you kidding?"

"We lived in a small town, Nick. There weren't any other Jews in West Alton then. I'm sure there are more now," she added with a bitter laugh.

Gwen said, "Nick, even in the late eighties, those old Yankees weren't about to muddy the waters letting their sons get involved with Jewish girls. Even the ones who weren't religious wouldn't allow it."

"Unreal," Nick muttered.

"We all dated, Nick, it's not like your mom and I were shut away," Gwen said, then added out of the corner of her mouth, "Well, Naomi didn't really go out much." She, too, had stopped pressing return address labels to the envelopes. "But we were social. It's just that it was a small town and pretty much all one flavor. There's prejudice everywhere, you know that. Even your father and mother had their share of...*concern* when they were first married." Cherry nodded but said nothing.

"From your parents, right, Mom?"

"You don't remember them, do you?"

"A little," Nick said. He put another invitation into an envelope and placed it on top of the pile in the middle of the table. "I have this one memory of them. Grandpa had a gray beard and Grandma smelled like cigarettes."

"That sounds about right," Gwen muttered.

"Your grandfather died when you were three, and your grandmother when you were five."

"Maybe Dad's parents will come to visit one day," Nick said with eyebrows raised.

"Maybe, honey." Cherry smiled and patted his hand. "We're fine now, Nick-Nack. Go ahead; your dad needs you at the restaurant. We're almost done here."

"Want me to wait and take the invitations to the post office?" Nick stood up, towering over his mother.

Gwen spoke. "I think we'll do that, Nick. I feel like taking your mom out to lunch today. Italian food."

✳

Joe picked up the phone and checked his watch. He dialed Suzanne's number and waited.

"Hello." The man who answered sounded pissed off. *Shit.*

"Hi, I was looking for Suzanne."

"This is her husband. Who are you?"

"Jake! It's Joe Traversa in California. From high school."

"Hey, Joe Traversa! How the hell are ya? How's life in Hollywood?" Jake laughed, a big, hearty laugh. Joe held the phone away from his ear.

He chuckled. "Life's pretty much the same everywhere, I guess, Jake. Hope I'm not bothering you."

"Nah, it's Sunday. Hot as hell here, though. You wanna talk to Suzanne?"

"If she's around."

"Yeah, hang on. She might be out back." Jake screamed her name and Joe held the phone farther away. "She's coming inside. You heading back for the reunion, Joe?"

"I think I might. If Suzanne is willing to go. What about you, you going?" Please say no, he prayed silently.

"Nah, not my thing, you know? Mine was two years ago, but I couldn't be bothered."

Joe understood. Jake had attended the vocational school down the hill, and everyone knew that voc-tech wasn't the same as high school. Jake probably earned more money working at Electric Boat than a Ph.D. college professor did.

"Joey! What a nice surprise!" Suzanne's sunny voice made Joe smile. "I hope Jake was nice to you. He hates talking on the phone."

"He's fine, honey. Listen, I had a crazy idea."

"Oh no, should I be nervous?" Her laughter reminded him of a carefree day at the beach. He should record it and replay it whenever he needed a boost.

"Ha. Listen, why don't you and Kellie come out for a visit before the reunion? You know, just the three of us, so we have a chance to spend time together and catch up. I'll fly you out. Maybe Labor Day weekend?"

"Really?

"I'm in this big empty house and would love the company, especially you two. Check with Kellie and let me know. Has she made a decision yet?"

"She's probably not going, Joey. She just can't see the point. I've tried; maybe you could convince her. She's been seeing someone, so I'll ask her if she can get away. What a great idea!"

"Well, I hope she changes her mind and comes with us. But all the more reason for the two of you to come out then. Find out and let me know, and I'll take care of the tickets."

"Joe, we can buy our own plane tickets!"

"No, I insist. Suzie, let me do this. Give an old guy a chance to spend it on his friends."

"I'll talk to her tonight." She hung up and turned around to see Jake standing in the kitchen, his arms crossed over his chest. "Joe Traversa invited Kellie and me out to California!"

Jake opened a can of beer. "Good for you, babe. When?"

Suzanne cut her eyes sideways to him. "He mentioned Labor Day weekend. You okay with that?" Would he be working that weekend? He hadn't said anything about it, but then again, he didn't say all that much these days, that is, when she saw him.

"Sure. I know we never go anywhere, and I can probably get some overtime."

"You work so hard," she murmured, moving to him. Tentatively, she put her arms around the man she'd been married to for twenty years. His belly pressed into her.

"Might as well make some extra money, right? When the work slows down, we'll have a little cushion."

She nodded into his neck. "As long as you don't mind." She realized she'd rather fly across the country to see her high-school friend than spend a long weekend with her husband. And that scared her so much it took her breath away.

Jake laughed, and the laugh turned into a cough. Suzanne drew a glass of water from the faucet. She handed it to him and he said, "It's Joe Traversa. I think I can trust you with *him*." He laughed again, and downed the water.

*

Kellie didn't fall asleep until almost four in the morning on Sunday. Scott Hunter had no idea who she was, of course, but running into him, literally, outside the restrooms, in that narrow, suffocating hallway at the back of the restaurant, well, it took all her oxygen away. She replayed the episode over and over again in her mind.

"Well, hello," he'd said in that ugly voice. Two simple words that came out sounding grimy and sweaty, because they had emerged from his mouth.

"Excuse me," Kellie had muttered as she tried to squeeze past him. He didn't back up against the wall to let her pass, though. And she would not let her body touch his. She could smell beer emanating from his pores.

He took a step to the side, just enough to block her path. "Please tell me you're not on a date."

She wouldn't look up. "I am," she said in the strongest voice she could muster. "Excuse me," she repeated.

He put his hand on her shoulder, and his sweaty palm made an imprint on her silk shirt. She drew back and raised her head. "Get out of my way," she commanded, pushing an elbow into his chest.

"Bitch," he cursed after her, loud enough for her to hear, as she hurried back to Bill.

"Please let's go," she whispered to him. She wouldn't sit.

"Kellie, what's wrong? Do you feel sick?" Bill rose to his feet. "We haven't ordered, but let me pay for the drinks," he said, pulling a twenty from his wallet and tossing it on the table.

She was already out the door.

He'd caught up to her on the street, and took her arm. "Please tell me what's wrong," he said.

"Just get me home," she snapped. She was silent in the car, thinking about what she would tell him. She couldn't tell him, not yet. And she certainly wasn't going to ask him to stay.

"Kellie," he said as he pulled up in front her building. "Please let me come in. I'll order a pizza, anything. But we need to talk about what just happened."

"I know we do," she sighed, and opened the door. Bill had parked on the street, and although he didn't need to feed the meter after six, he couldn't leave the car overnight. Back when their date began, she'd thought about letting him park in the underground garage, in her guest spot, but now everything had changed. He'd have to leave by midnight.

"Evening, Miss Kellie," said Kirby, standing behind his desk. "Sir," he added with a curt nod. His eyes never left Bill, Kellie noticed. She loved Kirby for that. Kellie smiled at him, mostly as a silent signal that she was fine.

Safely inside, Kellie turned the air conditioning back on. It was stifling in the room. She walked into the open kitchen and pulled down water glasses.

"I'm sorry you missed dinner," she said. Bill stood in front of her and held her shoulders. With one finger, he lifted her chin until she had to look in his eyes.

"I need to know what happened back there. You looked spooked even before you went to the ladies' room. Kellie, please."

If she didn't tell him, there was no way their new relationship could move forward. If she told him, he might think she was crazy. He might not ever want to see her again. He would wonder why an incident from twenty-five years ago should still bother her so much. Maybe if she just told him a little. She really liked him.

He let go of her shoulders and she poured water into two glasses, then brought them to the living room, where they sat side by side on the sofa. He turned his body toward her, bending his knee so his leg was partway on the sofa.

"I saw a man in the restaurant. Someone I knew a long time ago. And when I came out of the ladies' room, I literally bumped right into him." She gulped water, then mimicked his posture, turning to face him, bending her leg.

"What did he say to you?"

She shook her head. "He didn't recognize me," she said. "I look very different than I did when I was in high school," she added.

"A boy from high school who didn't recognize you? I don't understand. You practically ran from the restaurant, Kellie."

"I know, and I'm doing a very good job of explaining, I realize." She stood, walked to the window, kept her back to him. Maybe it would be easier if she didn't have to look into his kind eyes. "I recognized *him*. He didn't recognize me. He was not very nice in high school and those memories came back to me when I saw him. Even though he didn't know who I was, he tried to pick me up, outside of the restroom! And I know he was there with a woman. I saw her."

"Okay, Kellie. But your reaction to seeing this boy, this man, was more than simple annoyance. Enough that you bolted from the restaurant. He must have done something terrible to you in high school."

She felt him come up behind her. His arms encircled her waist and she squeezed her eyes tight. Twisting around to face him, she took a deep breath. *Tell him.*

"He assaulted me, Bill. Three days before graduation." She lowered her eyes and felt his arms tighten around her. She was confined within his embrace, and yet she didn't pull away. She was safe.

"Kellie," he groaned. "Did he rape you?"

She shook her head from side to side. "I'm sure that was his intent, but…no," she said, remembering. No, she thought, he was so repulsed by me that he threw me out of his car. She raised her face. "No, he didn't rape me." That was enough for now, she told herself.

Bill stroked her hair. Her cheek pressed against his cotton shirt. Clean cotton, she thought. Nothing better than clean cotton. Clean cotton, folded over itself so many times. Absorbent, clean cotton.

"I've defended a few criminals, you know. I could call someone, have him killed," he said with a sad smile. Kellie smiled back and kissed him.

"I'm okay, but tired. Sorry about dinner."

"Don't worry about it. I'll leave you to get a good night's sleep, dear. Okay if I call you tomorrow?"

"Of course. I want you to, Bill."

15

August 5 – 117 days to go

Suzanne sent a text to Kellie at five in the morning on Monday, but Kellie didn't see it until just before seven, when she woke after another night of just a couple hours of sleep.

Call me when you get this, Kell. Big news!

Kellie squinted at her phone. It was still dark outside, and the days were getting shorter, sunrise coming later. She'd shower first, try to wake up. It was going to be a long Monday with so little sleep.

After a cup of coffee, she called Suzanne and listened as her friend told her about Joe's call.

"Can you imagine? Kellie, we'd have a blast out there. Please say you'll go! Labor Day weekend. We could even fly out on the Friday, because it's California, and fly back on Labor Day."

"I'd have to ask Elizabeth. She might want me to work. And Bill…"

"Everything okay with you two? You sound weird."

"Very little sleep this weekend."

"Ooh, tell me all about it! Oh my God, is he still there?"

"Suzanne, please. It's not what you're thinking, not even close. We went to this restaurant Saturday, a Tex-Mex place, and Bill got up to go to the men's room. And right in my line of vision, Suzanne. Scott Hunter. I'd have known that face anywhere. And he was loud, that voice

106

like a chainsaw. I couldn't believe it. I mean, I was frozen in place. So Bill came back from the men's room, and I just, I was nauseated, I ran to the ladies' room, and there was nothing in me, only half a drink, but I was sweaty, and, it was awful, seeing him. I finally pulled myself together and I opened the door and I walked right into him."

"Oh my God."

"Well, he didn't recognize me. He started hitting on me! He was there with someone! He kept blocking my path, you know, it was this narrow corridor, and I couldn't get past him. Finally I just pushed him away and ran back to the table."

"Thank God Bill was there."

"Yeah, but I was freaked. I ran from the restaurant. Bill ran after me. Suzanne, I was shaking. The last time I saw Scott Hunter…"

"I know, Kell. I know. It brought all of it back. So Bill took you home?"

"Yeah. We never ate dinner. I felt awful. It had started out so well."

"But you told him, right?"

"Well, the best I could. I told him that the guy was someone from high school. That I looked different in high school and he didn't recognize me. And that he assaulted me three days before graduation. He asked if he'd raped me, and I said no."

"Did you tell him what he did to you?"

"I couldn't. Suze, we're still getting to know each other. I probably sent him running in the opposite direction with this episode."

"Well, he works with Ed, right? How much do you think Ed told him about your past?"

"I don't think Ed told him anything. Ed wouldn't do that. I know him, he wouldn't. And the whole story with Jonathan, that's just another chapter in the 'Kellie's Mistakes with Men' series. Oh my God, I'm a basket case."

She saw that it was getting late, and tried to dress while holding the phone between her ear and her shoulder.

"Stop. You're not, Kellie, and you know it. Listen, the same way Bill Hopeful told you about his wife, you can tell him about Scott Hunter. And your first husband. And even your short-lived second marriage if you want. Think about how hard it must have been for Bill to open up to you. If he could, then you can do the same for him." She paused. "If you want to," she tacked on at the very end.

"Okay, okay," Kellie said with a light laugh. "And I'll ask Elizabeth about Labor Day weekend. But I really have to go now."

"Great! Let me know as soon as you find out so I can tell Joey."

Kellie hung up and, before she resumed dressing for work, she pulled the CD from a shelf and slid it into a CD player that served as a bookend. She forwarded through the first nine songs until she landed on number ten, then she pressed a button on the remote. When her mother played this song on the old record player, she'd sing the harmony, the part Joni Mitchell sang. It was high, and Kellie couldn't sing it as well as her mom did. The song ended, and she hit repeat, and listened to it another seven times before she finally had to leave for work.

*

Kellie rapped on Elizabeth's office door and waited until her boss looked up and waved her in.

"A friend invited me out to visit in California for Labor Day weekend, and I was hoping to take a flight on the Friday of the long weekend," she said, standing in front of Elizabeth's desk.

Elizabeth frowned and made notations on the papers spread out on her desk. "We're so busy, Kellie, I don't know if we can spare you. The investigative team is planning a big story."

Of course they could spare me, Kellie thought. I do research. I could even do research from California. It's one day. "I haven't taken any vacation all summer, and it's just one day," she stated, trying hard to keep her voice from wavering. She hated that she let herself be intimidated by this woman.

Elizabeth looked up. "I know that, dear. Okay, go ahead and have your time off. We'll survive." She laid her fancy pen down and clasped her hands together. Today she wore red nail polish, as red as her lips. "Sit down, Kellie, please."

Kellie perched on the edge of the chair across from Elizabeth's desk. She bent her body forward and waited.

Elizabeth smiled, too broadly, those bright red lips a bloody gash across her face. "How's everything else going? Ed tells me Bill is quite smitten with you!"

Smitten? Who the hell says smitten anymore? And Ed would never tell Elizabeth something like that, even if Bill did say it, which she was sure he did not. Kellie pressed her bottom teeth into her lipstickless upper lip.

"Everything's fine, Elizabeth." Kellie tried to smile, but her mouth would not cooperate. "Just fine, thank you for asking. Is there anything else?" She stood before Elizabeth could answer.

"No, that'll be all." Elizabeth lowered her head to the papers in front of her and didn't look up as Kellie walked out of the office.

Back at her desk, she typed a quick text to Suzanne: *good 2 go pls tell Joe* and shut down her phone. She slipped it back in her purse and focused on her work.

*

Camille stopped by Kellie's office at the end of the day and invited her out for a drink. "I need something with alcohol in it!" she said, dramatically wiping her brow. Camille's lipstick had faded so that only the lines she'd drawn that morning still showed. "Please come with me, Kellie." She added, in a loud whisper, "I need to vent."

Kellie agreed, in spite of being dead tired. She dreaded spending an hour perched on a barstool listening to Camille complain, likely about her supervisor Myron. Myron was a good newsman but very old-school, and he had a habit of making remarks that came right up to the sexist line and danced all around it. Camille had complained about him once, and Myron received a verbal reprimand (and a wink, no doubt).

Kellie pulled off her jacket and draped it over the back of her chair. She kicked off her heels and placed them under her desk, then reached into her big bag for the navy flats she'd worn that morning. She stopped by Camille's desk and together they headed to the ladies' room to freshen their makeup. They waited in front of the elevator, and when the doors parted, they joined a young man who worked on one of the top floors. He grinned at Kellie and stepped to the side to let her in. She knew he'd never acknowledge Camille. Camille was invisible to him.

"All the way?"

"Excuse me?" Kellie stared at him.

"You're going all the way down?" He smirked and raked his eyes over her body. She turned to watch the numbers as the elevator descended. Camille stood silently, staring at nothing. When the doors opened, he gestured with his hand that she should exit first. She and Camille walked out to the lobby and the young man followed them across the floor to Arthur's, the restaurant and bar adjacent to the building.

He chuckled. "Let me get that," he said, reaching around her to open the door. His arm grazed her breast and she flinched without realizing it. "Are you…meeting someone?"

Kellie set her jaw. "I'm here with my friend," she said in a tight voice. Her facial muscles were so tense it hurt. He glanced at Camille and his smile faded.

"Too bad for me," he said. He couldn't be older than thirty, Kellie thought. He was attractive, but in a smarmy way some young men have, before their hair thins and they get the gut that won't go away. He practically walked with his crotch thrust forward, announcing to everyone that he had male genitals.

"Okay if we sit at a table?" Camille was headed toward one of about five tables set up opposite the bar. Kellie followed her; she didn't care for sitting at a bar, either.

They slid into chairs and Kellie noticed the guy from the elevator was seated on a barstool in her line of vision. Within a few minutes, he was joined by two other men and a young woman, who flipped her hair and tossed her head every time one of the guys said something. Kellie sipped her club soda and turned her attention to Camille.

"So, tell me what kind of day you had," she said. Camille sighed and began talking in a low voice, and Kellie had to strain to hear her over the loud, animated conversation taking place at the bar. The market, the projections, someone's mother, skiing in the Rockies. Blather.

"Do you think I should mention it to him?" Camille's shoulders sagged and she looked to be near tears. Kellie chastised herself for being distracted by the noise at the bar.

"Well…how would it make you feel if you did?" Good save, Kell, she said to herself. Now pay attention.

"Probably worse," she muttered. Kellie looked at the pink cocktail in front of her. She wondered if Camille really wanted a cosmopolitan, or if she ordered it because it was something she'd seen on television, or in a movie. As if drinking that pink martini made her feel more like the actress she'd seen sipping it.

"Hey, would you like to get some dinner?" Kellie asked. "We could move to the dining room, or even go somewhere else if you want," she added, with an eye to the young group at the bar. Yes, she'd rather be home, in her big, comfortable clothes, but Camille needed some company.

Camille wiped tears from her cheeks. "I'm so miserable," she said with a hiccup.

"Oh, Camille. Come on. It's never that bad," Kellie said, knowing that, indeed, sometimes it was. Sometimes it came down so hard, you thought your head might crack open. You wanted to fade into the earth, or be sucked up into the clouds. She knew. And the only thing she could offer to Camille was time and friendship. "Let's go somewhere else. You want to come back to my place and order a pizza?"

Camille raised her head. "Really?"

"Sure. At least we can put our feet up." She smiled at Camille, a woman who didn't fit society's definition of beautiful. And she never would. If Jonathan hadn't beaten me so badly that I needed plastic surgery, I'd still be that person, too. Kellie Blunt, the girl with the ugly nose and bad teeth. Camille wasn't unattractive. She just hates herself, Kellie thought. She needs to know that someone loves her. And that she's a beautiful person: kind, considerate, certainly capable of loving.

Camille paid the bill, insisting on it since Kellie only had club soda. As they stood to leave, Kellie glanced over to the bar and the guy from the elevator made eye contact with her. He grinned as his eyes skimmed her over and she turned away from him, letting Camille lead the way out.

"I wish I had my shorts with me," Camille said with a laugh as they entered Kellie's condo. "Wow, nice place!" She nodded her approval as she looked around.

"Hang on," Kellie called from the hallway. "I might have something." She returned with a pair of stretch yoga pants and tee shirt in one hand, and a soft cotton nightshirt in the other. "You can choose."

Camille rolled her eyes. "I can't wear anything of yours." She laid one hand on each hip and swiveled. "Unless those are big girl clothes." She laughed again, but

Kellie saw the apprehension in her eyes. She held them out.

"Try them," she said with a shrug. "If they're comfortable, you can wear them." She pointed toward the bathroom and picked up the telephone. "What do you like on your pizza?"

"Anything except anchovies. Whatever you like, Kellie," she called from behind the bathroom door. "I'm easy, ha ha ha."

Kellie placed the order and checked the refrigerator. Two cans of diet soda, age unknown, three bottles of beer, and a pitcher of water with lemon. That should suffice, she thought.

Camille emerged, wearing the yoga pants and a tee shirt that said "OBX" on it. She grinned. "I can't believe I got my fat behind in these. They'll be all stretched out now."

"I'm just glad you're more comfortable. Something to drink?"

"Are you drinking wine?" Camille eyed the bottle of red on the counter.

"A glass with the pizza would be nice, right? I ordered a large with green peppers and mushrooms." She poured two glasses of red and Camille followed her around to the living room, where they sat at opposite ends of the sofa.

"You have a perfect life, Kellie." Camille sipped her wine. "Can I be you for just a day?" She giggled again.

"You wouldn't want to be me. I think you're just fine being Camille."

"Are you kidding? You're gorgeous, you have great clothes, look at this condo. You wouldn't want to see my apartment, believe me. I bet you have a great boyfriend, too, right?"

Kellie wasn't sure about Camille. Likeable, unaffected, but Kellie trusted few people. And tonight wasn't about Kellie's life story, anyway. "I don't consider myself gorgeous. I probably spend too much money on clothes. But I am seeing a nice guy." She smiled into her glass.

"I knew it! Perfect life. Me, I eat too much, I still get zits at thirty-five, and I don't think I'll ever meet the right guy. And where do you meet them, anyway? Bars? Online? They all want someone 'slim and petite.'" She put a finger in her open mouth. "And I'll bet they're fat and bald."

Kellie's buzzer sounded. "That's the pizza. I'll be right back," she said, grabbing her wallet from her purse and opening the door. She took the elevator to the lobby, where Kirby stood next to the pizza delivery kid.

"Hey, Kirby," she said casually as she handed money to the boy. "Thanks." She took the large box from him. Kirby had already pressed the button for the elevator.

"You want to grab a slice before I head upstairs? I'll never tell."

Kirby chuckled and said, "You have a good night, Miss Kellie," as the elevator doors closed.

Camille stayed until after ten, oblivious to Kellie's stifled yawns. She seemed to be having such a good time that Kellie felt bad about calling it a night. She was sure that Camille would have stayed the night if she'd been asked.

"Well, I'll see you back at the office." Camille gathered up her clothes and Kellie handed her a cloth shopping bag for them. "I'll bring the bag back to you tomorrow, but I probably won't have a chance to wash these things until the weekend," she added, gesturing to her clothes.

"Camille, don't worry about it. Really. I don't even need them back." She opened the door. "Listen, Kirby will call you a cab from the lobby."

"Don't worry about me, I'll be fine walking. My apartment's not that far from here. Besides, no one messes with this girl," she said, laughing. Just before Kellie closed the door, Camille turned back. "I really had a nice time tonight, Kellie. Thanks for listening, and everything." She lowered her eyes as her cheeks flushed pink.

"I had a nice time, too. See you tomorrow." Kellie closed the door, locked it, and offered a prayer for Camille's safety.

16

August 9 – 113 days to go

Joe would have houseguests next month, and he was surprised at how excited it made him. Like a kid anticipating Christmas, he marked off the days until Suzanne and Kellie came to visit. He'd booked their flights and emailed the information to both of them. He'd arranged a car to pick them up at the airport, but would be there if he could. This weekend he'd go shopping for little extras to put in their rooms. It was going to be great to have people in the house again. Joe stepped into one of the extra bedrooms and decided it would be Suzanne's room. It faced east, and he knew she was a morning person. Kellie could have the room facing the ocean, next to his. He'd buy some hand creams and chocolates for his guests. It was going to be a memorable weekend.

The movie was wrapped, for the most part. Roberto Ozuna was involved with a starlet, a twenty-year-old girl who'd appeared in one of those vampire movies. They were on the cover of the tabloids last week, spotted together at the beach. But at least they weren't stopped for drunken driving or drugs. Ozuna was a well-mannered young man, Joe had to admit. Just heartbreakingly handsome. And so, so young.

He laced up his running shoes and was just about to head out the door when the telephone rang. He hesitated, debating whether he should answer it or let it go to voice mail. With a resigned slump of his shoulders, he stepped back inside and picked up the receiver.

"Hello?"

"It's your father. Your mother's in the hospital and it doesn't look good. You should fly out to see her before she goes."

That was it. So like his father. No emotion in his voice. Joe, on the other hand, tried to still his trembling hands.

"I'll be there as soon as I can," he said and hung up. Joe had learned that, with his father, short sentences were the way to go. He didn't even ask him for any other information; it wouldn't have mattered. His father was a man of few words, leaving Joe to get his answers elsewhere.

He stood staring at the phone before picking it up again. Please don't leave me, he prayed silently. Please don't die and leave me with him.

He lifted the receiver and called his assistant. "Monica, I need you to book me on a flight to Miami. As soon as possible. It's my mom," and his voice cracked on the last three words.

*

Flowers arrived just before noon. Kellie saw a pair of legs and a vase filled with colorful blooms in her doorway and laughed.

"Come on in, but don't trip," she said to Nancy.

"They just arrived." Nancy set the vase on a cleared space on Kellie's desk. "They're beautiful."

"They sure are." Kellie plucked the small white envelope and raised her eyes to Nancy, who stood waiting, smiling expectantly.

"I already know who they're from," Kellie said, twirling the little envelope between her fingers like a baton.

117

"And you're not sharing. I get it." Nancy chuckled and headed back out the door.

Kellie slipped the card from the envelope and read. *Thinking of you. Dinner tomorrow?* She tucked it back into the envelope and slipped it into her purse. The flowers took up so much space on her desk, she'd have to move them. Carefully, she lifted the heavy vase and set it on her side table. It was Friday, she thought. Why send flowers to an office on a Friday? I can't carry this home, and they won't last the weekend. She shook her head at the impracticality of it, knowing she shouldn't care. Even having them for the day was nice.

She leaned against the wall of her office, listening to the noises outside her door: a telephone rang, someone coughed. She picked up the phone to call Bill. It was lunchtime. She rang his office, reached his secretary, whose voice she recognized now, and who likely recognized hers. Bill wasn't in the office, but was expected back by three. Kellie asked for his voice mail and left a message. "It smells lovely in my office right now. Thank you, the flowers are gorgeous. And yes, dinner tomorrow evening sounds perfect. Call me later, either here or at home." She'd just ended the call when Camille appeared in her doorway.

"Hi! Did you bring lunch? Whoa, look at those flowers!" She clumped into Kellie's office and bent her head to the blossoms. Camille held the cloth shopping bag in her hand and offered it to Kellie.

"I didn't bring back the other stuff, because you said to keep them," she hesitated. "But this is your grocery bag."

"Thanks," Kellie said, taking the bag and sliding it into her bottom drawer. "I did bring my lunch today, and I think I'll just stay in here and work." She could have gone with Camille. It was Friday. But she didn't want to; she wanted to keep some distance with Camille. After bonding somewhat on Monday, Kellie needed to put some space between them. It's what she did with everyone.

Camille stood looking at the flowers. Kellie wondered if anyone ever sent flowers to her. Camille should receive flowers at the office. The other girls would be jealous.

"It looks like it might rain. I hope you have an umbrella," Kellie said finally.

Camille turned from the flowers and Kellie could see there was a stain on her dress, right below the neckline. A dark circle the size of a quarter. If that was from something oily, it would never come out, Kellie thought. "I'll just grab something downstairs. You sure you're all set?"

Kellie looked down at the mess of papers in front of her. "Thanks, I am." When she raised her head, Camille had moved to the doorway.

"Okay, then, I'll see you later." She turned away.

"Camille? Would you close the door, please?"

*

August 10 – 112 days to go

Joe flew to Miami, leaving Los Angeles before midnight and arriving just before eight in the morning on Saturday. He'd been able to sleep for a few hours on the plane, and after an espresso at the airport, was in his rental car heading to the hospital. St. Vincent's, of course.

As he sped along route 836, the Dolphin Expressway toward the hospital, he formed a picture of his mother in his mind. A mental image from the early eighties, his mom in a long maroon evening gown, her hair twisted up behind her head, dangling earrings that sparkled against her neck. His father, in his Marine evening dress uniform. Before they left, Joe took a photograph of his parents, so handsome in their best clothes. Then his father took his mother's arm and they went out into the evening, leaving Joe to play crazy eights with his aunt Shirley. Joe was in sixth grade, and he remembered caring more about his mother's clothes than his father's snappy uniform, with the navy blue coat and scarlet cummerbund. His mother, so elegant and beautiful he wished he could preserve her that way. He tried to keep that image as he walked into the hospital.

"Judy Traversa, please," he said to the receptionist. She gave him her room number and he speedwalked through the corridors to find his mother lying in a narrow bed. He stared. There was an oxygen mask over her mouth and thin plastic tubing above the blanket, stuck in her hand, her arm, her nose. A bag on a hook above her head, filled with clear liquid, dripping into her veins. Please don't die yet, mommy, Joe prayed silently.

"Ah, there you are." Joe stiffened at the sound of his father's gruff voice behind him. Atten-SHUN! Inspection time. He half-expected his father to grab his hand, check his fingernails. Joe turned.

"Hey, dad."

"You take the red-eye?" Joe nodded and turned back to gaze at his mother. "What happened to her?"

"Stroke."

"Will she wake up?" Still he trained his eyes on his mother, hoping his presence, his voice, might stir her.

"Don't know. Probably not." Joe heard the scrape of a chair as his father sat down. "I'da brought ya a coffee if I'da known you was here."

Joe inclined his head. "That's okay, I had a coffee already." His father was dressed in khakis and a short-sleeved shirt. His clothes looked clean and freshly-pressed, and Joe imagined his father ironed them that morning. Joe Senior did all the ironing, figuring he was the only one who could do it right. At least that was the way Joe remembered it.

"Yeah? Coffee? Or one of those fancy things? A la-dee-dah-tay." He slurped from a cardboard cup.

Joe walked out of the room, hearing his father mutter, "Oh, for Chrissakes." He approached the reception desk and asked the woman if there was another chair available.

"Sure, honey," she said, standing and pulling a beige plastic chair from behind the reception desk. He took it and smiled into her eyes.

"That's my mom in there," he whispered. "I don't think she's going to wake up, do you?" He just wanted to hear it from someone else, even if it was the same diagnosis his father had given. Maybe someone with a heart.

The woman touched his arm. "Your dad said you're a famous Hollywood movie director," she said. "He talked about you all day yesterday." She gave him a sad smile. "I'm so sorry about your mom."

Joe gripped the chair. "Thank you," he whispered back, as if he were in church, and carried the chair into his mother's hospital room.

17

August 10 – 112 days to go

Kellie cleaned her condo and changed the bedding. It was only dinner, she told herself, pulling off the sheets, extracting pillows from cases. We haven't reached that stage yet, she thought. But maybe we have. Maybe it's time. She stuffed the sheets and pillowcases into the washer and measured out liquid detergent, pouring it evenly over the sheets, dripping blue detergent on yellow cotton.

He doesn't even know about Adam. And that wasn't any kind of topic for foreplay. Still, if they were going to move forward, she'd have to tell him things. Things she kept to herself. Things she hated to talk about, to dredge up from the muck they lived in.

Bill arrived at six. Kellie had made a pitcher of Virgin Marys, and prepared a plate with olives and cheese. He looked nice, she thought. He had some color in his face and on his neck, although she assumed he had a golfer's tan, and wondered if she'd be seeing it later that night.

"Hi," she murmured into his neck. "Come on in." Kellie steadied her nerves. This was Bill. She tried to imagine how he must have felt when he told her about his dead wife. If he could bare his soul to her, lay it all out not knowing she had more than enough dysfunction to trump him, then she could be honest. Later.

"Well, this is nice. Look at what you did – a little snack before we head out?" His eyes twinkled and that dimple – there it was.

"Come sit with me." She took his hand and brought him to the sofa.

"Uh-oh, this can't be good." He laughed nervously but sat next to her, his thigh against hers.

Kellie took his hands. She lifted her eyes to meet his. "No, it is good, Bill. I want you to know how good this is. How much I like being with you." She heard him exhale. Actually saw some of the tension leave his body. "It's just that, you were very honest with me. About your wife. And I know that was difficult. I want to tell you a few things, too. And believe me, it's going to be really hard for me to do this, because I don't like talking about myself. About my past. But I know that moving forward means opening up." She let go of his hands and balled hers into fists, as if she was ready for battle.

Bill used his long fingers to slowly unclenched hers. He laid a palm over each hand and intertwined his fingers through hers. "Kellie, you tell me whatever you want to tell me."

She sipped her tomato juice and gasped. "Wow, I made this really spicy," she said, feeling the burn down her throat. She swallowed before speaking. "Okay, I was born and raised in West Alton. My mother and half-brother and I lived in a trailer." She kept her eyes on him and saw his eyebrows rise slightly. He wasn't expecting that, was he? But he said nothing; he just kept his fingers laced with hers.

"We were poor. My mother never worked, not that I know of. She was an artist," and Kellie whispered the word 'artist' almost reverentially. A special soul, a free spirit, an artist. "When I was about twelve years old, I asked her about my father, you know, who was he? Because I never met him. She told me that she went to Woodstock and met a man named Arthur Blunt. I was conceived there.

She met him on the way and they split up when the concert ended and he decided to stay in New York and work on the farm. He didn't know she was pregnant and she never wrote to tell him after she found out. So I only know these things about him because I asked, and she told me. My half-brother Adam was fathered by a man who stayed with us for a few months back when I was a kid. I called him Uncle Mack. Adam's seven years younger than I am." She tilted her head back and looked to the ceiling. After a long breath in and out, she said, "Adam is in prison, up at Walpole. He'll be there for a long time," she added quietly.

She felt Bill's eyes on her and faced him. "Wow, Kellie." Just wait, Kellie thought, it gets so much better. She tightened her fingers through his.

"You didn't ask, but I'll tell you anyway. Adam killed my mother. Our mother. He was a drug addict, and had moved away but apparently, he was in some kind of a drug-induced rage the night he tried to get her to give him money." Kellie let out a short bark of a laugh. "My mother never had any money. If he had been in the right frame of mind, he would have remembered that. From what I understand, Adam was furious when she didn't give him any money. He stabbed her twenty-two times." She glanced at Bill and his eyes glistened, shiny with unspilled tears. "I haven't seen or spoken with him."

They sat quietly for a minute or more, fingers intertwined, thighs pressed together, neither of them speaking.

"Kell." He seemed to be searching for the right words, but just as Kellie couldn't find them for Bill, she knew there were no right words, and besides, she had more to say.

"I was in my last year of law school when he killed her. In Chicago. I was working in Ed's law firm, and I worked closely with him. You probably knew that. I was married at the time, had been married for about seven months then, I think. My husband's name was Jonathan and he used to hit me." The more she talked, the more easily the words came, Kellie realized. She simply had to keep talking.

"I looked different back then. Not at all like this. I resembled my father, I was told. My nose," she said, touching her perfect, straight nose, "my nose was long and hooked, you know, like those witches in cartoons? It didn't have a wart, but it was ugly, that's for sure." Kellie felt as if she was levitating, rising slowly from the sofa, looking down on the handsome couple sitting close to each other on the sofa.

"My teeth were bad. Mom never took us to the dentist, so my teeth grew in all crooked. I never smiled, never showed my teeth." She ran her tongue over her smooth teeth. "Jonathan drove a delivery truck, but he also smoked pot, and they did random drug testing where he worked. He had to pee in a cup, and next thing, he was fired. That night, he came home, and he beat me up so badly I landed in the hospital. The neighbors heard it and called the police. He took off, and I was in the hospital when the police from West Alton were trying to find me to tell me about my mom. I hadn't shown up for work, and Ed tried to call me. Eventually, he and the police found each other and they told him what had happened to my mother, and what had happened to me. Ed came to the hospital. My face was pretty broken, my nose, my cheekbone. I'd lost a couple of teeth. So I had plastic surgery. And Ed stayed by my side. He was all I had back then. So, you can understand how special he is to me." She shrugged. "That's most of the story." Kellie leaned back against the sofa, drained. She hadn't ever told anyone the whole story like that, and it took more out of her than she realized. Like after the flu, when your body is battered.

"You poor girl," Bill murmured. He wrapped his arm around her shoulders and pulled her against him.

"I'm okay. Jonathan was charged with domestic assault, not attempted murder. I don't know if he was trying to kill me that night, or just get me out of his way. Do you need water or something?" Bill shook his head. He swiped a hand across his eyes.

"I really didn't want to come back here, to Rhode Island. After I got out of the hospital, Ed hired me back, which was fine, but I never finished law school. Then he started dating Elizabeth, who worked in Boston at the time. It was a real long-distance relationship and then things grew serious. I remember one day Ed invited me to have lunch with him, and he told me he was going to propose to Elizabeth. I was so happy for him. He mentioned that he'd probably be moving to Boston to be with her, and I tried not to cry, but you know, Ed was the only person I had, my one true friend, it seemed, and I didn't know what I'd do without him. But he wasn't going to just up and leave me. He'd spoken to Elizabeth and I went to Boston to interview for a job doing research at the television station. I was probably overqualified, but they hired me."

"So that's how you got your start in the news business," Bill said, popping an olive in his mouth.

Kellie nodded. "I worked directly for her. Doing research was a lot like what I'd been doing for Ed at the law firm. I'm very thorough, and I'm good at remembering details. And I really liked Elizabeth then." Kellie stopped. She cut her eyes to Bill. "I mean, I like her now, too." He smiled at her and she felt a warm flush on her neck. She really didn't like Elizabeth, but she was always careful not to let people think that. But Bill could tell. Maybe he didn't like her, either, maybe that's why he grinned.

"So I've been working for her for seventeen years now. Last year, as you know, Ed was relocated to Providence, and she moved here maybe a month or two after that. And once I had completed some of the projects I was working on in Boston, they moved me down to Providence this past spring. I don't know," Kellie mused, holding a piece of sharp cheddar between her fingers, "sometimes I think they still feel the need to keep an eye on me. Ed especially. He's like a big brother. Very protective."

Bill chuckled at that. "Why is that funny?" Kellie asked, seeing his merry eyes.

"Protective is the right word," he said. "When you and I started dating, Ed pulled me aside one day and gripped my upper arm. He leaned his face in close to mine and said, 'If you hurt her, I'll kill you.' He growled it, like he was a mobster or something. He said, 'She's like a sister to me, you know.'"

Kellie grinned. She'd told him enough of her past for tonight. "I'm starving," she said. "I guess I worked up an appetite with all that talking."

"How about that steakhouse on the west side?" Bill stood and extended his hand to her. When Kellie placed her hand in his, he pulled her to her feet, then drew her close and wrapped his arms around her. "I know that was hard, and it meant a lot to me that you felt comfortable enough to share it."

"Let's go," she said, glad she'd changed the bedding.

*

It was Scott's weekend with Tara, and he didn't want her taking up his two days any more than he knew she didn't want to be there. Why couldn't they just be honest with each other and not bother? He'd send her some money and she could do whatever the hell it was she did during the summer. It wouldn't kill her to work, either, he'd told Laurinda on the phone the previous day.

"Scott, get a clue. Maybe next summer. Modeling or something."

"Modeling? She's a kid. It's bad enough you let her dress like a slut..."

"Shut up. You're no role model for our daughter. I'll drop her off in an hour." The next thing he knew, she'd hung up on him.

Shit. He sighed loud enough for the neighbors to hear. And all Tara ever wanted to do was hang out at the mall. Maybe he'd just drop her off, hand her a couple of twenties, and pick her up four hours later. He wouldn't mind finding that little porker Molly for some action. Yeah, that might work. But he didn't have her number, didn't know her last name, and it wasn't like he could walk across the parking lot to the other building and start ringing doorbells.

Scott lifted his bare feet and rested them on the wicker table. A hot breeze blew over his face, and he wiped the sweat from his forehead. Tara will want to sleep in his room, with the air conditioner, and he'd end up out here on the deck again. Not that he minded. And maybe he'd see Molly and her friend. He chuckled. Will couldn't get out of the house; Ellen had him on a short leash ever since last month, when they picked up those girls at The Fool and Will crawled home after midnight, smelling like perfume. Ellen threw a few things around the kitchen, mostly the china that was his mother's, and almost locked him out of the house that night. Now he was kissing her ass every day *and* every night. Scott shook his head. Better him than me, he thought. Liz never found out about Molly. And Molly, after that night, well, he figured if he was going to see her again, he'd have to apologize. Obviously she didn't want to do everything, even if she had led him on. He could have kinky sex with Liz anytime. Skinny Liz with those sharp bones. Molly was like a soft body pillow.

He sank lower in the wicker chair, into the old cushions that smelled faintly of mildew. Maybe a quick nap before Tara shows up, he thought, closing his eyes. Because then it's game on until Sunday night. I gotta get down to Florida, he thought. Before Christmas. Right after the reunion.

*

128

Cherry received an email from Suzanne Fitch. Oh, Suzanne Fitch Thomas, she read on the monitor, jotting Suzanne's married name on a pad she kept next to her computer. In the email, Suzanne thanked Cherry for organizing the reunion, said she would be attending with Joe Traversa, and she asked Cherry if she'd sent an invitation to Kellie Blunt. Cherry frowned at the computer. Kellie Blunt? Kellie Blunt. Oh! Kellie Blunt. Crap, she'd never thought about Kellie Blunt. Her yearbook was on the floor next to her computer; she opened it to the back, where all the senior pictures were in alphabetical order, small black and white photographs of girls with long curly perms, boys with sculpted hair. No Kellie Blunt. She wasn't there.

Cherry tried to picture Kellie Blunt in her mind. Long hair? Dark? She absentmindedly smoothed over her eyebrow, where tiny hairs had sprouted back. Her fingers traveled along her face, down her cheek. Kellie Blunt. When her finger reached her nose and she touched the tip, her eyes flew open. Kellie Blunt! The nose! Yes, she remembered. Oh, that poor girl. The nose, the bad teeth. The clothes her mother made her wear, like a hippie from the sixties. Cherry didn't think she'd said two words to Kellie Blunt the entire time they were in high school. And Suzanne must know her.

She typed back a reply: *"Hi Suzanne! Thank you for reminding me about Kellie. Because she wasn't pictured in our yearbook, I had missed her. Of course I would like to include her, and I hope she can attend the reunion. Do you have contact information for her? I'll send something out right away. Thank you so much, and I'll see you and Joe in November! Cherry Weiss-Patel*

After proofreading her words, she sent the message and sat back. Kellie Blunt. Suzanne wants me to send her an invitation, but Cherry couldn't imagine the poor girl would attend. Unless, like Joe Traversa, she was now rich and famous. And (God forgive me for this) better looking.

Cherry slipped a hand under her shirt and touched the scars. Two angry red lines swiped across her chest. Her breasts, her marvelous, lovely breasts were gone, and she was being mean about Kellie Blunt. Shame on me, thought Cherry.

18

August 11 – 111 days to go

Kellie opened her eyes and saw Bill lying on his side, his eyes half-open as he watched her.

"Morning," she murmured, her voice still full of sleep.

Bill reached out and pushed her hair back from her face, and lightly grazed her cheek. "Good morning, beautiful," he said. His chin was stubbly. She touched it and felt the roughness.

He pulled her closer. "How are you doing this morning?" His fingers tickled her back.

She didn't know how to answer his question. She wasn't sure how she was doing. Being with him last night was good. No, it was better than good. Maybe she didn't recognize this emotion. Hope? Hope that their relationship would continue to grow, to strengthen? Hope that he felt the same way about her? Hope that the feeling, of hope, would conquer the dark times of despair?

"I'm doing great," she said.

Kellie didn't know if he was satisfied with her, physically, and she was afraid to ask, which she knew was ridiculous. She'd held back, unable to let herself go, and that was partly because she hadn't told him everything. And yet, last night, after they'd returned to her place, the timing wasn't right to talk more about Scott Hunter. She figured she could get around not having that discussion, but now she knew it was an obstacle. It would always be an obstacle until she was able to blast it to pieces.

"Coffee? I need some," she said. He released her and grinned.

"Mind if I shower?" He rolled out of her bed and stood up, comfortable in his nakedness. She watched him walk across the floor to the bathroom. He looked pretty good, she thought. Strong thighs, wide shoulders. Bit of a soft belly, love handles, but that made him more real. Once he'd shut the bathroom door, Kellie swung her legs over the side of the bed and pulled on a long terrycloth robe. She cinched the belt around her waist and padded into the kitchen to make coffee. Opening the refrigerator door, she grimaced. I need to make breakfast for him, and I've got nothing. Four eggs, okay. She opened a cupboard and found a jar of sun-dried tomatoes in olive oil. She set it on the counter and continued searching.

Kellie set up the coffeemaker and listened to him singing, and she closed her eyes for a moment. Uncle Mack used to sing in the shower. Sometimes her mom would sing with him, from the kitchen. Her mom sang all the time, in a voice that was as sweet as any of the singers she'd try to imitate.

There was some shredded cheese in the freezer, and a bag of chopped spinach. I can make a decent omelet with this, she thought. But there's no bread. Oh, well. I'll slice up this orange to fill the plate. It'll be fine. He knows I'm not much of a cook, she reminded herself.

As Kellie put together the makeshift omelet, she remembered how she'd get creative with what little food there usually was in the trailer. Her mother was always distracted by a new project, and never remembered to shop for food. It's not that she didn't care, Kellie knew that. Her mom would get involved, so involved she'd forget about everything else. When Adam was little, Kellie bathed him, made sure his clothes were clean, his tiny teeth were brushed, his hair was combed. She'd walk to the farm, where old Henry would sell her eggs and stick his tongue out at her. He told her once he'd give her a dozen eggs for nothing if she lifted her blouse. Kellie had hurried back to the trailer, but never told her mother. Next time she had to go there, she took Adam with her. Old Henry wouldn't dare try anything with a little boy present. Then one afternoon she came home from school and there was old Henry, sitting out back with her mom, in the rusty chair that wobbled back and forth. One of his hands held a cigarette and the other one rested on her mother's knee. He never even said hello to Kellie, and she went straight to the back of the trailer to study. But a few days later it prompted her to ask again about her father.

"What do you want to know, Kellie? I told you his name last week, remember?" her mother had asked. She was sitting outside in the afternoon sun, painting what looked like the ocean on a large piece of canvas. The entire canvas was blue, with one strip at the top a little lighter blue than the rest. She hoped her mother would add something to it, like a boat, or a whale. Kellie was twelve. Some of the kids at school had parents who were divorced, but they all spent time with their dads. They all knew their fathers. She sat on a wooden crate next to her mother and rested her elbows on her knees.

"His name was Arthur Blunt."

"That's right. Everyone called him Artie, though." Her mother stopped painting for a moment and turned to face Kellie. "You really want to know about him?"

Kellie nodded and pushed her hair out of her face. She wanted to know everything about him.

"Okay, well, I told you about Woodstock. You should write a report about it sometime in school, because I was there, I could help you with it. Remember when I told you about it? I wasn't supposed to go, but I went anyway. I disobeyed my parents," she added with a meaningful look. "I got a ride with some kids from college. Artie was hitchhiking, and even though we didn't have room, we picked him up near Worcester. I had to sit on his lap, so we started talking, you know?"

Kellie nodded, even though she'd never really talked to a boy. The boys at school didn't even look at her.

"And all the best singers were performing that weekend," her mother continued in a dreamy voice. Her eyes were far away as she spoke. "Everyone was happy, everyone got along. There were drugs, but not everyone was taking them. It rained, and no one really cared. Artie and I wanted to spend some time together. It was just so easy then. Love was free and it was easy." She was silent for a long time and Kellie hoped she wasn't finished.

Free and easy love sure sounded nice, Kellie thought. Her mother picked up her paintbrush.

"I just wish my name was Kellie Campbell. Not Kellie Blunt."

Barbara held the brush like a cigarette. "I wanted to name you Wheat. Isn't that a beautiful name?" She laughed, tossing her head back as if she was laughing at the sky. "Kellie, you were conceived in the mud, for God's sake! You're Kellie Blunt, and it's a great name."

Kellie disagreed, but she didn't want to tell her mother why, because she didn't want to say the name that Scott Hunter called her. So she nodded.

"My parents were very angry with me when I arrived back home. And a couple of months later, I found out I was pregnant. With you," and she pointed the blue-tipped paintbrush at Kellie, almost touching her nose.

"Did he come to visit one time? I remember a man coming to visit when I was little." Kellie rocked back and forth on the wooden crate. "He brought a jar of peanut butter."

"No, honey," her mother said, and Kellie saw her face slacken, her eyes fill with sad memories. Kellie wished she hadn't asked. "Your father never knew about you, honey. It was a difficult time. My parents were upset, I was scared.

And Artie, well, Artie was working on the farm." She stared at the blue canvas.

Kellie thought it wouldn't have been so hard for her mother to write to him at the farm, to at least tell him that he had a little daughter. But she knew when she had asked enough questions. Her mother had resumed painting, and Kellie rose from the wooden crate and went inside.

The sound of Bill opening the bathroom door snapped her back to reality. Wafts of steam drifted out and dissipated in the cool air. He stepped into the kitchen with a white towel wrapped around his waist. His skin was pink and his wet hair was combed back from his face.

"Are you making breakfast for me? I would have taken you out." He eyed the skillet on the stove.

Kellie refocused her attention, where her omelet was beginning to set. She turned to Bill. "It'll be ready in a minute. There's an extra robe in the closet – it's white and it's big," she added.

His laugh filled the kitchen. "I was hoping for pink and ruffled." He disappeared into the bedroom.

Kellie set the small table with white plates. She found cloth napkins in a drawer, yellow and red, and folded them, placing one next to each plate. She set a mug beneath the Keurig and filled it for Bill, then refilled her own mug, and brought the steaming coffee to the table. She divided the omelet onto the plates, giving him most of it, and finished by layering thin slices of orange around the edge of the plate. It didn't look bad, she thought.

Bill emerged from the bedroom wearing the big white robe.

"Did you steal this from a hotel?" he asked with teasing eyes.

"No, I bought two," she said with a laugh.

"Just in case?" He tilted his head slightly, and Kellie blushed. They sat down and Bill dug into his omelet. Kellie wished she'd had bread for toast. Now she'd have to start keeping food in the house to feed him. Well, if he comes back, she thought.

She pushed her tongue around inside her cheek and looked up at him through her eyelashes. "Bill, I moved to Providence in February. You're the first man to stay over. Just so you know," she added and looked at her plate. She picked up a slice of orange and bit into it.

He set down his fork and placed his hand over hers. "Look at me, Kellie." She lifted her chin. He leaned in and kissed her softly on the lips. Their eyes were just inches apart. "Thank you for telling me. I want us to be exclusive with each other. I love being with you."

Kellie swallowed hard. She was expecting to hear something completely different and now she didn't know what to say. "Me too," she whispered. She wouldn't say anything more about Scott Hunter. Not when everything was so good.

*

August 12 – 110 days to go

By Monday morning, Judy Traversa's condition hadn't changed. Joe and his father met with the physician, a small woman who looked too young to be a doctor. Joe peered at her lab coat. Dr. Tariq was embroidered in blue thread. He glanced nervously at his father, praying the old man wouldn't make a crack about her ethnicity or her gender. But Joe Senior sat stoically and stared at the far wall until the doctor coughed softly.

"I know this is very hard for both of you," she began in unaccented English. "We had hoped she might show a sign of improvement over the weekend, but unfortunately, nothing has changed. At this point, she is alive only due to the respirator and feeding tube."

Dr. Tariq waited and observed Joe's father, whose expression hadn't changed.

"Dad," Joe said, "you understand that, right?" He reached out to lay a hand on his father's arm, but Joe Senior jerked his arm away and rose to his feet. He stood ramrod straight. Of course, thought Joe. Don't let any emotion get in the way.

"You've done everything for her, is that correct? Nothing more to be done?"

Dr. Tariq tilted her head back far enough to look up at Joe Senior. "Yes, sir." It was as if she knew how to answer the ex-Marine.

"So, what now? You pull the plug?"

Joe winced and bowed his head.

"With your consent, we would remove the naso-gastric tube that provides liquid nutrition. Use of the ventilator is a quality of life decision."

"There is no quality of life!" he yelled. Joe saw his father's fists clench and the veins in his neck stand out like ropes. "She might as well be dead now," he muttered. He stuck his hands in the pockets of his creased khakis. "She might as well be dead."

Joe left the room and paced the area in front of the nurses' station. He was due back in Los Angeles for a post-production meeting. Pulling his phone from his pocket, he telephoned his assistant and explained the situation in as few words as possible. She said she'd reschedule for the end of the week. Then he returned to the room and sat by his mother's bed.

"It's your decision, dad," he said softly, pressing his lips to his mother's lifeless hand.

When he left the hospital, he returned to his hotel room, and his father returned to his condo. No dinners together, no reminiscing about the good old days – what good old days? Separately, they each waited for Judy Traversa to die.

19

August 16 – 106 days to go

Scott sat on his deck and opened his third beer. The humidity was oppressive and he wished he'd taken his bike to the beach. Maybe he'd go pick it up from Will's shed this afternoon and head south for the evening. No one around to see him.

He scanned the parking lot, looking for Molly's car, but it still wasn't there. Yesterday, he saw her Indian friend, whatever her name was. He'd run down the stairs to get to her before she went inside, calling "Hey!" because he couldn't remember her name.

She'd turned, frowned, and was about to turn away when he said, "Listen, I just want to talk to her. Please let her know."

"She told me all about you."

"I'm sorry, I'm trying to remember your name."

"Maya," she spat out in disgust.

"Maya." He ran a hand through his hair. "Maya, listen. I'm not a monster. I really like her. It was a misunderstanding between us, all my fault. I want to send flowers, but I don't even know her last name, or what apartment you live in."

Maya narrowed her eyes at him. "You don't even know her last name?"

"She never told me! Look, you know we all had a lot to drink that night. I want to make it up to her, take her out for a real date, maybe to the beach or something. At least let me send her flowers."

Maya stood, one hand on her hip, and considered. Finally she said, "Molly Hanson. Apartment 2-E."

"Thanks. Really, thanks," Scott said, and ran back upstairs. He called a florist and ordered a dozen red roses to be delivered to her the next day. When the florist asked him what he'd like to have written on the card, he said, "Um, just write, 'I'm sorry. Scott.' No! Wait. Make that, 'I miss you. Scott.' Yeah, that's it. Thanks."

This morning, he'd seen her white car parked in front of her building, and he'd been sitting on his deck when the florist delivery truck eased into the parking lot, looking for building C. It stopped and Scott watched the driver hop out, open the back door and pull out a glass vase filled with a dozen red roses. He watched the driver walk up to the building and ring a bell, then he saw him enter the building and come back out, minutes later, empty-handed. He waited for his phone to ring all morning, but it didn't.

Well, what the hell, he thought angrily. He just spent fifty bucks on flowers and she wasn't even going to call him? He took a shower, just in case she'd want to see him, and when he emerged from the bathroom, shaved and clean, her car was gone. He kicked the refrigerator and almost broke his toe.

Now it was mid-afternoon and still her car was gone. Well, screw her, Scott thought. Plenty of fat, grateful girls around. Fat girls were easy. He'd take his bike down to the beach. He decided to drive to Will's, leave his car and take his bike out of the shed. Then he'd ride it back to the apartment so that when she finally returned home, she'd see it. Perfect, Scott thought. He stood up and wobbled a bit, but downed the rest of the beer and grabbed his keys from the table. He stumbled down the stairs and got into his car.

He made it to Will's house without incident, and laughed to himself. Not the first time I've driven buzzed, he thought. He parked on the side of the house and noticed Ellen's car in the driveway. He shut off the engine and opened the car door, and heard loud music coming from the house. A couple of the windows were open, and Scott remembered they didn't have central air, just a unit in the bedroom upstairs. He stood outside the house and listened. Driving beat, a song from high school. He couldn't remember the group, but they kept singing 'relax.' He edged closer to the house and caught a glimpse of Ellen dancing through the house, light on her feet, wearing her underwear. Scott stood transfixed, watching from the driveway, hoping to see her again. What was she doing in there? He felt a stirring, listening to the pulsating music, imagining Ellen.

"What are you doing?" A high-pitched voice behind him caused Scott to jump. He turned to face Kelsey, Will and Ellen's daughter. "Why are you looking in our windows?"

"Uh, I heard a noise. I was just coming to get my motorcycle," Scott stammered, not looking at the girl.

"Mommy!" she called. The music had stopped.

"Just a minute, honey! I'm getting dressed!" Scott imagined Ellen again, slipping a sundress over her toned body. He glanced at the girl, who continued to stare at him with her small eyes and stupid braids. She wouldn't know Scott; he wasn't included in their cook-outs and pool parties. Ellen barely tolerated Will's friendship with him.

He walked quickly to the shed and rolled his bike out. Just as he jumped on the seat and gunned the engine, Ellen opened the side door and stepped out. She was barefoot. Scott noticed a thin gold chain around one ankle, and bright red polish on her toes. He raised a hand in greeting and revved the bike, then sped away from the two of them.

Scott chuckled to himself on the way back to his apartment. That little twerp kid of theirs, she'll end up being a bitch just like her mother. He took a turn back into the apartment complex and rode right past the unmarked white van parked in the lot.

*

Joe sent a text to Suzanne, letting her know about his mom. *Check ur email*, he wrote. He'd told her, in his message, about his mother, and indicated that she'd probably be pronounced dead that weekend. He had to fly back home on Saturday either way. And he was still expecting them over Labor Day weekend. *I need to see you two now more than ever*, he wrote.

He pushed back from the hotel room desk and stood. The days were growing shorter already, he noticed. That time of the year, mid-August, always brought on a sense of melancholy he couldn't explain. Perhaps it was the shortened days, or the memories of back-to-school shopping with his mother. Maybe it was remembering a late-summer vacation from many years past.

His father always took the last two weeks of August for vacation, and for a few years, the three of them had rented a cottage at the beach. Nothing fancy, just a small house with paneled rooms and lumpy furniture. Joe didn't care, though. He swam in the ocean every day. He walked the beach with his mother, their heads bent down, looking for shells, or sea glass, or a starfish. In the evening, they'd have hamburgers or hot dogs on the charcoal grill, or clam chowder from the take-out place down the road. Even his dad seemed more relaxed. He'd have a beer and laugh with the neighbors, act like a normal person.

The summer Joe was thirteen was the last summer they'd spent at the beach house. There were new neighbors that year in the house next to them, a pleasant family from Massachusetts with two kids, a girl who was sixteen and could drive, and a boy a year younger than Joe. His name was Ronald, but everyone called him Skip. And the way Joe's heart wobbled in his chest when he first saw Skip, he was pretty sure he had his first real crush.

141

Joe looked around at his hotel room and knew he needed to get away from it. He wanted to go to the beach, so he closed the hotel room door behind him and walked toward the ocean. The area was lit up and crowded on a hot summer night, and Joe needed to be among the living; he wanted to soak up whatever energy they were emanating. He walked down to the beach and sat on the sand. People were everywhere, he noticed, but it wasn't strange for him to be sitting cross-legged on a beach at night. Not here.

His mind crawled back to Skip and the friendship they shared that summer. Neither of the boys really understood what was going on. Their parents were pleased that their sons had become friends, and thought nothing of them going out at night to walk along the beach. And when they returned, each to his own cottage, sweaty and red-faced and covered with sand, their parents simply told them to take a shower before getting into bed.

On the last afternoon at the cottage, Joe said with measured nonchalance, "I'm gonna go next door, see if Skip wants to go swimming one last time."

"Be back for supper," his father called, snapping his newspaper.

Joe ran over to Skip's cottage and the boys headed to the beach. They swam out to the jetty, where the big rocks served as a spot for the fishermen to cast their lines at dawn. There were no fishermen there that day, though, and Skip and Joe were able to swim to a small cove that was hidden from view. There, they splashed and horsed around and kissed. And Joe had never known anything so exquisite in his entire life. The feel of Skip's soft full lips against his own was almost more than he could bear, and his hands groped under the water. The boys lost track of time.

Apparently, an older woman had seen the boys splashing in the water, then didn't see them at all. There were no lifeguards in the area, and the woman recognized one of the boys as Joe Traversa's son, from the yellow cottage, and ran to find him. Joe Senior ran down the jetty, over the large, flat rocks. He ran ahead of the old woman, so he was the only one to see. His looming figure blocked out the sun, casting a shadow over the two boys, and young Joe looked up first. Even in silhouette, he knew it was his father. He pushed Skip away harshly, yelling at him, calling him a queer. He swam away as fast as he could, never looking back until he reached the shore, where his father stood waiting, arms crossed, aviator sunglasses hiding his eyes.

"Get your towel," was all he said, and Joe picked up his towel, leaving the one belonging to Skip, a green towel with bright pink watermelons on it, lying crumpled on the sand. He cast a glance back to the jetty in time to see Skip trudge out, his head down, his shoulders hunched toward his skinny chest. And a piece of his heart was ripped away then, the first piece of many.

The noise from the café on the beach brought Joe back to the present. He leaned back on his elbows and stared up at the sky. There were constellations, but he'd never learned them, and the sky just looked like an inky mass with specks of stars. He rose to his feet and walked back to the hotel.

*

Kellie stopped to pick up her mail late on Friday afternoon, and was surprised to see a letter with a return address from Mrs. Cherry Weiss-Patel. Suzanne must have done that, she thought. She shook her head and entered the elevator.

Bill had invited her out on his boat for the weekend. The forecast was good, plenty of hot weather still left this summer, and he'd suggested going to Block Island. He'd pick her up early in the morning, so she was grateful for a night to herself. Plenty to do, but first she'd telephone Suzanne.

"Hey, you," she said. "Guess what the mailman brought today?"

She heard her friend chuckle on the other end. "You should at least have an invitation," Suzanne said. "I still think Joe and I can convince you to go. We'll work you over in California."

"Ha," Kellie said. "Well, I'm still not sold on the reunion, but I am excited about going to California."

"I heard from Joe. Well, by email. His mom had a stroke in Florida last week. She isn't going to recover. They took her off the respirator; now it's just a matter of time."

"Oh, I'm so sorry," Kellie said. She closed her eyes and saw her own mother, paintbrush in hand. "Is he still in Florida?"

"Yeah, but he has to leave tomorrow. He needs to get back to LA. Poor Joe. I'm sure he was hoping his dad would go first."

"Suzanne…"

"You know what I mean. His father's a prick, always has been as far as Joe is concerned. And Joey's such a sweetheart, what's he going to do, just abandon his father? I feel bad. But he was insistent that we both still come out next month."

"Okay, if he's sure. But I'd understand," Kellie said. "Listen, Bill's coming to pick me up early in the morning. We're going to Block Island in the boat."

"Ooh! Weather should be great this weekend."

Kellie murmured her agreement. "What should I take? I can't overpack."

"One pair of shorts, one pair of long pants, a couple of tee shirts, a sweatshirt, your bathing suit, and underwear. Kellie, it's a boat, you won't need much. Really, your bathing suit might be enough." She laughed.

"You know, we've shared so much in the past weeks. This weekend, it feels right. I'm not nervous about it at all."

"About time, sister. Just kidding. I'm glad, Kell. And I'm glad you've told him everything."

"Well, just about. He probably knows enough about Scott Hunter even though I didn't tell him the whole story. I just feel as if there's a hole that needs to be filled."

"Well, let Bill fill it. Oh, you know what I meant."

"Yeah, yeah. I'll talk to you later." She tried to keep her voice light. Maybe Bill did know enough. Why go over the whole horrible afternoon again, just to add details? Details would only burden him, and she didn't want to burden him.

*

Scott pulled into his parking spot and hopped off the bike. He turned his head and saw Molly's white car in the space across the lot. Good. He jogged across the parking lot and pressed the buzzer under her name. As he waited, he stretched his back and glanced over his shoulder at his bike, gleaming in the afternoon sun.

Molly answered the door, wearing a sundress not much different from the one Ellen had been wearing. It was snug across her belly and hips, though, and Scott let his eyes linger on her chest. Her skin was white where her bathing suit straps must have been, two thin white lines rising from her breasts to her neck.

"Hey," she said with narrowed eyes. She pursed her lips and shifted her weight to one foot so her hip jutted out. "Thanks for the roses. They're beautiful." She dipped her chin. He lifted it with a finger and waited until she looked at him.

"I feel awful about the way things went between us. It was my fault; I totally misunderstood. And if you're not into that, it's okay. All I can do is ask you to forgive me.

I've missed you so much." He traced his finger along her bare shoulder and watched her shiver.

She licked her lips, her plump pink tongue darting in and out of her mouth. Was she trying to torture him? "You know, I don't like it rough. You were rough with me."

He turned his palms up. "Honey, I had way too much to drink that night. That wasn't the real me." He used his head to point back to the bike. "I wanted to make it up to you. Take you to the beach on my bike." He watched as she gazed past him to the shiny motorcycle across the lot. It winked at her in the sun.

"That's yours? Wow," she breathed. "I love bikes." She tugged at the strap of her sundress.

"Come on, Moll, let me take you to the beach. We could get a bite to eat, watch the sun go down, maybe even go swimming?" He gave her his best sad puppy look.

It worked. She cracked a smile. "All right, fine. Let me just put on my bathing suit." She turned away from him.

"I'll run upstairs and get my stuff and meet you at the bike in five minutes, okay?"

"Kay," she called and he ran across the parking lot and sprinted up the stairs.

20

August 19 – 103 days to go

Joe was back in Los Angeles, and his mother hadn't died yet. He'd had a conversation with Dr. Tariq before he left, saying only that he'd like to be able to call her for a status report. He didn't mention anything about his father, but he sensed that she knew. Of course she knew; wasn't it obvious to everyone? Anyway, she'd promised to call him with any news.

So he tried to focus his attention on work. They had finished shooting, and were in post-production. It would likely take several months to complete, but Joe had the best editors, sound, and special effects people around.

Len Troope had phoned while he was in Florida, and he owed him a return call, or a text. Joe rested his head in his upturned palm. Len Troope. There wasn't any chemistry there, at least not for Joe, and he didn't want Len to believe something that wasn't true. Besides, they were on opposite sides of the country. And, and. He tried to list all the reasons why it wouldn't work. There was just something about him. Sure, he looked great, he was attentive, definitely interested. And then Joe realized what it was. Len wasn't Paul. No one would be Paul. And Paul wasn't coming back. He hadn't heard a word from him since he'd left in June, but one of the assistants on the set mentioned that she'd run into him up in Santa Barbara a couple of weeks ago. Joe had simply nodded and smiled. He wouldn't ask.

Instead, he dialed Len's number and waited for the cue to leave a message.

"Hey, Len, sorry I missed your call. I was in Florida to see my folks. My mom..." as he realized his voice was about to break, he stopped and took a deep breath. "She had a stroke, and she's going to die very soon. It's been rough, so I'm sorry I didn't call. I'm around." He ended the call and broke down sobbing. He wouldn't see his mother again; he'd said goodbye privately at the hospital. At least his father had left the room so he could be alone with her.

*

Cherry's follow-up visit with her oncologist was first thing in the morning. She wrapped the *dupatta* around her head before leaving the house with Gwen. They drove in near silence to the doctor's office, Cherry lost in her thoughts. She implored a God she wasn't even sure existed to kindly give her a good report. No more cancer. Please. And then He, or She, could ask for something in return, something Cherry would be happy to give. A kindness, a sacrifice.

Gwen swung the car into a parking space and turned off the air conditioning. Just before Cherry turned to slide out of the seat, Gwen held her forearm. Cherry looked in her eyes and wondered if her own fear mirrored back to her sister. "Everything's going to be fine," Gwen said with authority. Cherry smiled back, as if she believed it.

"Thanks, hon. I believe it, too."

Seated on a vinyl-covered chair in the waiting room, Cherry crossed one leg over the other and bounced her foot.

"Do you want a magazine?" Gwen offered her one with a photograph of salad on the cover.

Cherry shook her head. "They're covered with germs," she said. She smoothed the *dupatta* on her head.

"What isn't covered with germs?" Gwen asked, and started flipping through pages.

When the nurse called Cherry's name, Gwen touched her arm again. "Okay by yourself?"

"Perfect. I'm fine," she said before walking from the waiting room. The door closed behind her and she followed the nurse down a long corridor to an examination room. Everything so neutral, she thought. Soft lighting, shades of beige on the walls, the floor, the furniture. Was this supposed to make her feel calmer? Because it wasn't working, she wanted to tell someone. Try some nice, bright colors if you want to cheer people up, she thought.

She entered a small examination room and changed into a cotton gown without being asked. She knew what to do. She held the material tightly against her chest, until the scars were visible through the thin fabric.

Dr. Sing entered the room with a brisk 'good morning' and Cherry laced her fingers in her lap. She thought he looked grayer this morning, or maybe she just hadn't noticed before.

"Cherry, how are you feeling? You look good," he said. "Your hair's growing back?"

She touched the *dupatta* again. "A little," she replied, never taking her eyes off his. But he looked down, at her file. He fidgeted. *Tell me*, she screamed silently at him. *Tell me it's all gone.*

"Well. We removed both of your breasts in a double mastectomy, but cancer can still return to the area. The more lymph nodes with cancer at the time of the mastectomy, the higher the chances of breast cancer recurrence. In your case, we found a lump in your chest wall."

Cherry heard a shrill whistle, like a train whistle from an old locomotive roaring through her head. She couldn't hear Dr. Sing; she could only watch his lips move. She held up a hand and he stopped speaking.

"I'm sorry, I missed that last part. Would you repeat it, please?" She sat very still.

The doctor leaned forward and rested his arms on his thighs. She noticed his wedding band was silver. Maybe it was platinum. "Cherry, your first breast cancer was treated with mastectomy. Now the cancer is back in the chest wall, so we want to perform surgery to remove the new cancer. There may also be cancer in the lymph nodes, so I will remove some or all of them under your arm. We may also use hormone therapy. Do you understand?"

"Do I need more chemo?"

He shook his head. "Not right now. Let's get you scheduled for surgery. Now, who's out there with you? Bud?"

"My sister Gwen," she said in a tiny voice, like she was seven years old again. "Bud's working." Her body felt as if it was filled with sandbags, like someone kept adding more and more weight inside her until she couldn't move. The cancer was back, he'd said. Well, get it out, she wanted to scream. Three months until this reunion. I will live until then, she vowed.

*

Kellie was back at work on Monday morning, sleep-deprived, a little sunburned, but happy, for the most part. The weekend on Block Island had started out choppy but had a smooth ending. If only she hadn't brought up that stupid reunion. Alone in her office before her colleagues arrived, she reflected on what had gone wrong.

They had arrived at the marina under a cloudless sky on Saturday, and Kellie couldn't wait to be in the sun and on the water. She'd bought a wide-brimmed straw hat to shade her face. As they unpacked Bill's car, he said, "You're awfully quiet this morning, Kellie. Is something bothering you?"

"I've never been on a boat. Well, I know I've been on yours before, but not for a weekend. Not all the way to Block Island."

"Nothing to worry about. We'll take it nice and easy." He chuckled. "I remember my first time on a boat. My uncle John took me out when I was fourteen. He taught me how to sail." Bill looked out into the distance, and Kellie looked that way, too. She looked for Block Island, but could see nothing but water. "Anyway," he said, closing the car door, "let's start our day."

Kellie pulled her two bags, Bill grabbed a bag and a cooler, and they made their way down the dock to the boat. It was a beauty, Kellie had to admit. It was named 'Kick Back,' which Kellie believed to be simply Bill's way of relaxing, until he explained that a wealthy doctor had basically paid for the boat when Bill defended him against kickback charges.

"He paid for this boat?" she'd asked.

"His legal fees paid for this boat. He was under indictment for fraud, and I defended him."

"Was he guilty?"

Bill smiled. "He was found not guilty by a jury."

She thought about that. "So you got him off."

"He was entitled to a defense, Kellie. I provided that defense. The prosecution was unable to prove guilt beyond a reasonable doubt."

"Okay," she said, and gave him her best smile. They weren't even out of dock yet, and already she was tense. She didn't want to argue, certainly not about some rich crooked doctor.

"Well," he said, picking up the bags, "I'll get these put away and then we'll head out."

Kellie followed him below deck. "So, I've got a high school reunion coming up in November."

"No kidding," Bill said, laying her bag on the queen-sized bed that was tucked under the bow. He continued to unpack groceries, filling the little refrigerator and

151

cupboard. He looked at her. "Are you asking me to go with you?"

Kellie felt a warm flush, the heat creeping up from her neck to her scalp. "Oh, no, actually, I wasn't. I didn't think you'd want to go. I don't even know if *I* want to go. You know, high school." She wished she could be more blasé about it.

Bill finished putting away the food, and slid the cooler under the table. "High school. And what about that man you ran into at the restaurant? The one who had you so worked up? Do you think he'll be there?" He locked his eyes on hers.

Kellie took a deep breath before speaking. "I don't know. My best friend Suzanne is going, and her friend Joe. Joe Traversa, he's a movie director in Hollywood. They both want me to go with them." She wished she hadn't brought this up at all. But he stood there, waiting. She sat on the edge of the bed.

"Why are you telling me this, Kellie, if you're not asking me to go with you? If you don't even know if you're going? You don't need my permission to go to your high school reunion." He moved to sit next to her.

She tucked her hands under her legs. "I don't know why. I guess, well, we've been so honest with each other, and I wanted to let you know about it, and that I'm not sure about it." She looked up at him. "We haven't even started our weekend and I'm bringing up a stupid subject like a high school reunion." She had that thickness in her throat, like she might cry, but she would not cry.

Bill pulled her hand out from under her thigh. "You brought it up because it's been on your mind ever since you saw that thug at the restaurant, right?" She nodded. "Is there anything else you want to tell me, Kellie, before we head out?"

Kellie looked away, considering. Would it ruin the entire weekend? Probably. She turned back to him. "I told you I looked different back then. And why I look different now. I'm just worried that if I go back, if I attend this reunion, no one will recognize me, and then when they learn who I am, they won't even remember me. And Scott Hunter will be as mean and rotten as he was twenty-five years ago."

"Kellie, it's a reunion. It's supposed to be fun. If it's not going to be enjoyable, I can't imagine why you'd even consider going. Revisiting our past isn't always easy, but it shouldn't be so daunting that you can't function. When is this reunion, anyway?"

"Late November."

"All right, then. You have time to decide. If you want me to go with you, you know I will. But if it causes you this much anxiety to think about seeing your high school classmates, I'd think seriously about whether it's all worth it. Okay?"

She nodded, feeling like a complete fool. Like a teenager, like the old Kellie Blunt. She just hoped she hadn't ruined what promised to be a great weekend. "You're absolutely right. I don't even want to think about it right now."

"Good." He squeezed her knee. "Let's get out onto the water. Come on, you're my first mate."

And she didn't think about it all weekend. They glided over water that was as smooth as glass and anchored at the island by mid-afternoon. Kellie stared in awe at the bluffs as Bill gave her a brief history lesson. They swam and biked and ate grilled bluefish that was brought in on the afternoon fishing boat. At night, she was rocked to sleep by the motion of the boat on gently undulating waves.

Bill suggested they motor back earlier than planned on Sunday, as the weather was building to the west and he didn't want them to be caught in a storm. Choppy waters greeted them on the ride back, but Kellie never felt seasick. She loved every minute of her time with Bill.

She emerged from her reverie by the sound of her colleagues arriving at work. Telephones and copiers and coffeepots and another week was underway.

*

Monday morning brought a good start for Scott Hunter, too, because he'd had an exceptional weekend. Molly was a tiger in the morning, and knew just how to wake him up. Unlike Liz, who usually rolled to the side, lit up a stinky cigarette and puffed away while he made coffee, Molly was an attentive little thing who pleasured Scott, then got out of bed and made him coffee and breakfast while he showered. And she knew when to leave, too.

"I gotta go," she said. "I want to shower and change before classes."

She never asked when he'd call, never tried to make plans. Scott was surprised; he figured a girl like Molly would be more desperate, more needy. On Friday, she'd ridden behind him on his bike to the beach. He took her to the Clam Hut, where they drank beer and ate fried clams at a picnic table outside. They ran into the ocean and he lifted her to his shoulders, her weight displaced in the water. Then they'd walked on the beach until the sun went down, and she'd let him put his hands under her shirt. She climbed back on the bike and tightened her grip around his waist, obeying his order not to touch him anywhere else. By the time they'd arrived back at the apartment complex, it was late. When he left Molly's apartment on Saturday morning and walked across the parking lot to his own place, he didn't even look to his right, or he might have seen the white van, but Scott was feeling good. Tired and spent, but pretty damned good. He sprinted up the stairs to his apartment and slept away the morning.

In the early afternoon, he brought the bike back to Will's house and was relieved that no one was home. Still, thoughts of Ellen dancing around the house in her underwear returned to his mind, and he called Liz that afternoon.

"I'm sick," she said.

"You don't sound sick."

"I've been puking all day, Scott. All I wanna do is sleep. You're on your own tonight."

He forgot to tell her to feel better and hung up. She might have been lying; he could never be sure with Liz. He phoned Molly but she didn't pick up, and her car was gone when he looked out from the deck, so he ordered a pizza and polished off a six-pack. Then he watched some porn and fell asleep.

On Sunday, he walked right across the parking lot and rang her bell, and when she opened the door, he grabbed her waist and picked her up.

"What are you doing?" She giggled and kissed him on the mouth.

"I'm making dinner for you tonight," he said, puffed up like an old toad. "I'm a great cook!"

He saw her eyes shift to the side, as if maybe she was looking for someone's car in the parking lot.

"Hey, no big deal if you have plans."

"No! Dinner sounds great." She raised her hands above her head, an odd gesture, he thought, almost like a signal. "I'll bring a bottle of wine." She smiled sweetly at him.

"Come up around seven. Bring red wine." He leaned down to kiss her and stuck his tongue in her mouth a few times, then kneaded his fingers into her lush behind. He turned and jogged back across the parking lot, and never saw Mollie give a thumbs-up to the white van.

21

August 20 – 102 days to go

Tuesday was anything but boring for Kellie. Elizabeth caught up with her as she entered the building and said, "I hope you're ready for a big adventure, Kellie."

Kellie didn't know how to respond. "Uh, sure. Always. What are you talking about?" She stepped into the elevator with her boss and the doors closed.

"I have a special project for you. It'll take up most of your time, probably even some weekends," she said, twisting to inspect the heel of her shoe.

Weekends? This better not mean Labor Day weekend; Elizabeth had already told her she could have that time off.

"What is it?" Kellie felt a queasiness in her stomach. Her jaw muscles tightened.

"Come to my office as soon as you're settled. We'll talk there," she said, striding out of the elevator as soon as the doors parted. Kellie was left standing outside the glass doors to the station, speechless. She turned to go inside and was nearly knocked over by Camille, who had just turned a corner. She held an empty coffeepot in her hand, and the round glass carafe hit Kellie square in the chest.

"Oh! Sorry, Kellie. Why am I always the one to find the coffeepot empty?" She laughed. "Oh well, I'll be back. And you and I can have a fresh cup." Kellie watched as Camille retreated, her skirt too tight across her backside, the hem higher in back where her ample bottom claimed more fabric. I don't have time to wait for coffee, Kellie thought. She hurried to her office, changed her shoes, tucked her lunch bag into her desk drawer, and walked down the corridor to Elizabeth's massive office.

"Come in, sit down," Elizabeth said to Kellie, and stood to shut the door behind her. That was unusual, Kellie thought; Elizabeth liked her office door open. As Kellie waited, Elizabeth shuffled some papers. *Is she going to fire me?* Finally, her boss looked up and smiled.

"I have a special project for you, Kellie." Her phone buzzed and Elizabeth let out an exasperated, exaggerated sigh before picking up. "Yes," she stated into the receiver. "Send him in." She looked at her diamond watch and frowned.

Kellie turned as the door opened and Jeff Braun walked in. Jeff was the station's investigative reporter and probably one of the best in the business. He was thorough and fair, not one of the many 'gotcha' reporters out there today. He looked as if he'd just rolled out of bed, and Kellie thought maybe he had. Jeff was known to work late, and thought nothing of working weekends.

"Morning," he mumbled, taking the chair next to Kellie. "Sorry I'm a little late."

Elizabeth let her eyes rest on him for a moment, but said nothing. She respected Jeff, Kellie knew it. The station's ratings were high mostly because of Jeff's work. "Good morning. You know Kellie. I've brought her in to assist you on this new project. Would you like to explain it?"

Jeff raked a hand through his hair, which only managed to make it more tousled. It worked on him, though, Kellie thought with a small smile. With a glance at her, he began.

"We're doing an exposé on fake disability claims by state and municipal workers. It's going to be an ongoing series, and we're starting with civilians, then working to police and fire. The state's going broke paying these claims, and we know some of them are false. But most of these people have corrupt doctors willing to state they're permanently disabled. So we've had a couple of guys doing undercover surveillance for the past six weeks, and when we televise the injured parties doing things that a disabled person shouldn't be able to do, well, we've got 'em."

Kellie considered this. "What kind of things are they doing?"

Jeff sat forward, animated now to talk about his project. "Well, we have this one woman who said she hurt her back lifting a box at the office. That was four months ago. She's out on disability – temporary, but it's been four months and the department says they don't know when she'll be able to come back. We filmed her playing in a softball league last week. Swinging a bat, running after fly balls, sliding into third. Great stuff." He grinned at Elizabeth, who caught Kellie's eye and gave her a 'see, told you' look.

"Anyway," Jeff continued, "I asked Elizabeth here for some backup help. My guys are working all kinds of crazy hours doing surveillance, and I need someone back here in the office who can keep everything organized: the film, the reports, maybe get the background stories. And she suggested you." With that, he leaned back in his chair and clasped his hands together behind his head. Kellie noticed faint yellow stains in the armpits of his shirt. He must live alone, she thought.

"So, Kellie, this is an exciting project. Jeff plans to begin the exposé at the end of the month with the woman he just described. His team is gathering film now, because once these reports air, everyone will be on guard. You're filming all month, right?" She looked at Jeff.

"Yeah, we're almost done. We're on a firefighter right now. It's great stuff. My guys have him jumping on his motorcycle, riding all over the place. They even got him giving his girlfriend a piggyback ride. How do you do that with a permanent back injury?" He spread his hands and held his palms up while making an exaggerated face. Kellie actually laughed.

Elizabeth picked up a stack of papers on her desk, a signal that the meeting was over. "Any questions, Kellie, see Jeff. And track your extra hours." When Jeff stood up, Kellie noticed a bit of red on his shirt. She hoped it was ketchup.

After Jeff had exited the office, Kellie stayed behind. Elizabeth looked up and pursed her lips. "What is it?" Her tone was clipped.

Kellie began, "It's a great project, Elizabeth. Thank you for thinking of me." Elizabeth nodded and looked back down at her papers. "It's just that, you'd already told me I could take Labor Day weekend off, and I made travel plans." She waited, steeling herself for the expected eruption.

"Work that out with Jeff," she said curtly. "You report to him until this project is over." She lowered her head again and Kellie knew she was dismissed.

"Thank you," she said and practically skipped out of the office.

*

August 30 – 92 days to go

Kellie called Suzanne as soon as she woke up.

"What? Kell, it's five in the morning," Suzanne rasped. "What's wrong?"

"Listen, I have to go in to work early so I can leave early. I'll meet you at the airport at three."

"Jeez Louise, Kell, you're going to work? I thought we might hit the spa today, get all prettied up for Joey." Kellie heard the bedsprings creak on the other end.

"Can't. Jeff is letting me off this weekend only because Elizabeth had already promised me. He didn't want me to go, but I begged. I gotta run. See you at three."

"You'd better be there!"

Kellie disconnected the call and laced up her running shoes. The sun wouldn't be up for another hour and she had to make her way through darkened streets to the station across the river. She probably should have called a cab, but there wasn't time for that now. She could run if she had to. Her bag was packed, so as soon as she ran back home in the afternoon (after skipping lunch), she'd get a taxi to the airport.

Across the street, the empty lot remained untouched. There had been no construction all summer, which meant the developer still hadn't come up with any money. She knew a couple of homeless men camped out there, because she'd seen them from her fifth floor window. She crossed the street to the far side of the lot. Kellie picked up the pace when she heard papers rustling. In an effort to save money, every other streetlight had been shut off. She caught a flare of light out of the corner of her eye. Was that a flashlight? The sky in the east was lightening to gray.

"Hey!" A voice was behind her, a ragged, gravelly voice. A voice like sandpaper. She didn't care. Run, her head screamed, run. Kellie ran as fast as she could, over the bridge, through the little park, and she reached the station office building, breathing so hard she thought she might pass out. The front doors were locked and she pounded on the glass until the security guard ambled over. He stood there, on the other side of the locked doors, staring at her until she pulled her ID card out and held it up for him to see. Finally, he unlocked the doors.

Without a word to him, Kellie panted her way to the elevator and punched the button. She wouldn't turn around until she was inside and the doors were closed.

*

At ten minutes to three that afternoon, Kellie's taxi was racing south down the highway to the airport. Suzanne had an hour's drive north from Mystic, but she'd told Kellie that her daughter Skye was back from camp and would drive her. Good, Kellie thought, I haven't seen Skye in forever. The driver pulled up to the departures area and Kellie said, "Delta, please."

"I drop off here," he said in a thick accent.

"You can't pull up to Delta?" She looked at his eyes in the rearview mirror. He gave her a dark, hateful look. Or was that just her imagination?

"I drop off here," he repeated.

"Fine," she snapped. She slid out of the taxi and waited for him to pull her bag from the trunk of the car. The fare was $28.63. For once, Kellie was determined not to overtip. He could have pulled up, she told herself, and there weren't any barricades or anything. She waited until he'd placed her bag on the curb before handing him thirty dollars. He snatched the two bills from her hand and muttered something unintelligible before getting back in the cab and peeling away.

Kellie rolled her bag into the terminal and walked the distance to the Delta counter, where she saw Suzanne standing with Skye. As Skye ran toward her, Kellie forgot all about the mean cab driver and embraced the girl who now stood as tall as she did.

"Look at you," Kellie said, touching Skye's cheek. "You're all grown up. How did that happen?" Skye grinned at her. "And the braces are off! Wow!" Kellie just shook her head. "Back to school?"

"This weekend. Can't wait, actually. Sorry I kept missing you all summer."

"All right, sorry to break this up, but Kell, we have to go," Suzanne interjected. Kellie hugged Skye and whispered to her, "I'll see you soon," then handed her off to her mom, who kissed her and slipped her some money.

"Put gas in the car," she said. With a wave, Skye jogged to the exit doors.

"Come on, let's go," Suzanne said, pulling her bag behind her. "You don't have to check that, do you?"

"No," Kellie said. "I fit everything in here. Are you excited?"

Suzanne bobbed her head. "I can't wait to see Joey. And I think it'll be good for him to see us, after losing his mom."

"Did he fly back for the funeral?"

Suzanne shook her head, and her earrings, which were small brass coins strung on silver wire, bounced against her long neck. "She was cremated. His father just did it, no service or anything. At least Joey had a chance to say goodbye," she added, then scrunched up her face in regret. "I'm sorry, Kell. That just came out."

Kellie patted her friend's arm. "It's okay. I'm glad to get away for a few days."

"Everything okay with Bill Hopeful?"

"Oh, sure. He was happy for me. We see each other on the weekends, but during the week, we're just busy. It's nice to talk with him on the phone, and when I see him, I'm happy, you know? I guess it's enough for now. He seems to be satisfied with things as they are."

"Are *you* happy? I mean, would you two ever move in together or anything?" They inched through the line, making their way to the scanners.

"I don't see it, at least not now. I love my place, and it's the right size for me." She turned to Suzanne, who was pulling her driver's license from her wallet. "I failed at two marriages. Definitely not looking for a hat trick," she said with a short laugh. "Besides, I'm sure he isn't thinking about that."

Suzanne shrugged. "No one's getting any younger here."

"Yeah, well, things are fine, and I'm looking forward to this weekend." She didn't say, *shut up already.*

They moved through the screening process without incident, and headed to their gate.

"We stop in Atlanta, you know," Suzanne said, making a face.

"I'm not complaining, and you'd better not be, either. Come on, first class to LA, chance of a lifetime." She pulled her friend's arm. "And as many drinks as you can slide down your throat."

. .

22

August 31 – 91 days to go

After a delay in Atlanta, Delta flight 2524 touched down just after midnight. Joe tossed aside the magazine he'd been reading and uncrossed his legs. He hadn't seen either Suzanne or Kellie since high school, although Suzanne had sent photos over the years, so he was pretty sure he'd recognize her. All he knew about Kellie from Suzanne was that she looked very different.

He recognized his old friend immediately. Suzanne's pale, angular face hadn't changed, he thought, as the two women walked into the arrivals lounge. He raised a hand in greeting and she rushed him, like a slender linebacker, dropping her bags to the floor and throwing her arms around him.

"I can't believe this!" she cried, hugging him harder. No one looked at them; this was Los Angeles, and everyone had their eyes peeled for celebrities. Joe Traversa didn't qualify, apparently. And he was grateful tonight for that.

When Suzanne finally let go, he took a step toward Kellie. She held her hand out to him and offered a shaky smile.

"Hi, Joe," she said. He couldn't say if Kellie's voice was the same; in all the time at high school, he'd heard her speak less than a dozen words.

He took her hand and pulled her to him. Screw it, he thought, they're both my friends this weekend. He felt her stiffen slightly in his embrace, but only for a brief moment, then she relaxed and he felt her arm encircle his waist.

He was careful not to make a big deal about her appearance, per Suzanne's instructions. "Welcome to Los Angeles, ladies. Finally, right?"

"Joey, you are one gorgeous man, I gotta say," Suzanne said. "The years have been very kind to you."

"Right back at you," Joe said, glancing at Kellie. "Both of you. Come on, the car's here. You two must be exhausted." He led the way out of the airport and a shiny black town car pulled up, right on cue. The driver put the bags in the trunk and the three of them climbed in the car. Joe couldn't stop smiling.

*

Summer drifted into autumn. The change was more subtle than in New England, but even in Malibu, there were signs of transformation. Sunrise was later, sunset earlier, and the morning air was sharp and crisp. Joe chose a long-sleeved tee for his morning run. The girls were already up, still not adjusted to the time difference. It didn't matter, they'd told him the previous night over a glass of wine, by the time they were used to it, they'd be heading back east anyway. He stood on his deck and watched them on the beach. Kellie and Suzanne stood close together, their backs to him. Waves lapped at their ankles, but neither of them flinched, and Joe smiled. My hardy New England girls.

How wonderful to have life in his house again. He'd wanted to stay up all night with them, laughing and talking, but after one glass of wine, he could see they were both ready to crash. He'd shown them to their rooms and called good night, then sat outside by himself for another hour. At five-thirty, after a few hours' sleep, Joe heard them in the kitchen. They'd all need a nap later in the afternoon.

He'd spent the entire summer without anyone. Well, except for Len Troope. He didn't want a relationship with Len; it would never work. A couple of his friends offered to introduce him to someone they knew, but he'd refused, telling them he wasn't ready. Now he was ready. It hurt too much to spend every night alone, and he missed the warmth of another body next to his. Paul was gone, and Joe knew he had to put him out of his mind for good. Last week, he'd taken the photograph of the two of them and hidden it in a drawer. Out of sight, maybe one day out of mind.

He finished his stretches and turned back to his friends. Suzanne talked with her hands; she was animated as she spoke to Kellie. Kellie Blunt, or, Kellie Campbell, as she was now known. Talk about a metamorphosis. Of course, he knew the reason she looked so different, and he could still see sorrow in her eyes. Perhaps it was being with high school friends that dredged up old memories. She put up a good front, but Joe knew all about barriers. About not letting too much show, even with good friends. Suzanne was not only Kellie's best friend, she was Joe's best friend, too. But even with that link, he never knew much about Kellie.

Joe knew her story from Suzanne. He knew she was brought up in a trailer on the edge of the Watson Farm, with her hippie mother and her younger brother. He recalled the handmade clothes that were so far out of fashion: muslin skirts, tie-dyed tops. Her big nose, her bad teeth. Poor Kellie Blunt. He didn't know about her first husband and the abuse until Suzanne had told him, but he had to admit, her face was beautiful now. She'd been put back together and emerged a very pretty woman. Still, you couldn't change those eyes.

They were waving at him. Jolted back to the present, he waved his arm over his head and ran down the stairs to the beach.

"I'm going for a run," he said when he joined them on the wet sand. "Anyone want to join me?"

"Nope," Suzanne chirped. "But I will take a dip." She shrugged off her shorts and tee shirt, revealing a toned body clad in a black tank suit. "Kellie, come on!"

"Later," Kellie murmured, watching Suzanne jump into the ocean like a kid on the first day of summer. She loves life, Kellie thought with a twinge of envy. Wait, I love life, she reminded herself. I just don't have the same abandon that she has.

"Okay, then, I'll be back," Joe said. In a lower voice, he added, "The house is open, so don't go too far." He took off down the sand at a leisurely jog.

He left the house open? Kellie was shocked. She watched Suzanne duck her head under the waves and wondered if she should go back up to lock it. I know this is a good community, she thought, but leaving the house unlocked? That's just nuts.

*

September 1 – 90 days to go

On Sunday evening, after an exquisite dinner of grilled mahi mahi, and as Joe uncorked the second bottle of wine, Suzanne made a suggestion.

"I think you could use two assistants, Mr. Traversa. We would require little; just a view like this and grilled fish every night. We could move in right away."

Joe raised his glass. "I'm all for that," he said, winking at Kellie. "This house is too big for just me, anyway." He refilled their glasses and leaned back, looking up at the sky. "I love this time of day, just after sunset and before dark. Dusk."

"The gloaming," Kellie pronounced it. "Tranquil peace." She, too, tilted her head back.

"I thought you were a morning person," Suzanne said in a too-loud voice. She gulped down the rest of her wine and reached for the bottle. Joe watched her with a bemused look on his face. "Miss Suzanne Fitch, I do believe you are tipsy," he drawled with a southern accent.

"Stay there, you two, I'll clear these away," Kellie said. She stacked plates and carried them into the kitchen.

"Just put everything in the sink," Joe called from the deck. "I'll deal with them in the morning."

"You should have a maid." Suzanne's voice was sloshier.

"I had Paul," Joe said, looking into his glass. He looked up. "Should I open another?"

"Let's switch to something else. Whaddaya got?"

Joe laughed. "Everything," he said. "What do you want?"

"Everything," she said with a laugh. "I want this life. I have more in common with you and Kellie than I ever had with Jake." Suzanne's lips twisted as she considered that last statement.

Joe knew she was drunk. *In vino veritas*, right? But she was also his friend, and he wanted her to know that she could tell him anything. He glanced into the kitchen, where Kellie was rinsing the dishes.

"Jake's good to you, though, Suzie, right? He'd never hurt you. *Right?*"

She picked up Kellie's glass of wine and drank all of it down. "He's never home. He pulls as much overtime as he can at the shipyard, and he stays with his buddies in Groton. When he comes home, he sleeps. We have enough money, he doesn't need to work so much." She looked up at him with shiny eyes. "We haven't had sex in almost a year. Well, I haven't. Maybe he has, I dunno." Her head wobbled.

The thought had crossed Joe's mind, too, but he wouldn't give it any weight. "I doubt that. Jake loves you, Suzie. Hang on." He left her for a moment while he retrieved a few bottles from a cabinet. "Kellie, get back out here this instant," he called good-naturedly.

She raised a hand and called back, "One second, I'm coming."

Joe placed three bottles on the table. "I have bourbon, scotch, and this liqueur. It's tequila-based. I've never tried it." He looked up as Kellie rejoined them. "Come on, Kellie, have something with me. Suzie?"

*

Three hours later, Joe and Kellie had put Suzanne to bed. They relaxed in lounge chairs on the deck, sipping scotch and gazing at the stars.

"Are you still on the fence about this reunion?"

"I guess so," she said, running her index finger around the rim of the glass. "I'm so happy to be spending time with you and Suzanne, but the others?" She lifted her shoulders. "I just don't see the point." She turned her face to him. "What about you? Why go back after all these years?"

Joe was silent for a long time, and Kellie thought perhaps she'd offended him with her question. Finally he spoke.

"I think I need to. I need to face my past. Because it still haunts me." He rubbed his face. "Did Suzanne ever tell you what happened? Right before the senior play?"

"No, not that I remember. You were Pippin! Joe, you were so good in that show. Did something bad happen?"

She heard Joe's intake of deep breath. He swung his legs around so he was sitting on the chair, facing her. Realizing that he had a story to tell, she did the same, her knees almost touching his as they faced each other in the dark. The deck was lit only by the flame of a candle, and light flickered across Joe's handsome face, giving him an almost ghostly appearance.

"The play was in early April, and we had rehearsals almost every night. The night before we opened was dress rehearsal. I'd changed out of my costume and back into shorts and a tee shirt, but I still had my stage makeup on. I didn't bother to take any of it off. My mom had the car, so I was waiting for her to come pick me up. I remember it was drizzly, chilly outside, you know how sometimes in the spring it's still cold? The other kids had all left and I was standing outside the school entrance, waiting. Shivering. My mom was late that night. Usually she'd be waiting in the car when I got out of rehearsal. Some nights I drove myself, but we only had one car, so that night I was waiting for her and she was late. Then I saw headlights approaching, so I started walking toward the car." He straightened his spine and ran his hands through his hair.

"Where's my drink? Here," he said, taking a huge gulp. "I need fortification to tell this story," he said with a short laugh. Kellie sat and waited; an involuntary shiver skittered across her skin.

"It wasn't my mom. It was Scott Hunter, and Will Blake and Robbie Jordan in Will's Monte Carlo. Scott was driving, but they all looked pretty wasted. He rolled down the window and said, 'What are you looking for, faggot?' His words were all slurred, you know? One of them, Robbie I think, told me to get in the car. I said no, I didn't need a ride. I didn't want any trouble with these guys, they were all bigger than I was. He yelled at me. *'Get the fuck in the car!'* I started walking in the opposite direction, but Scott gunned the car into reverse, and Robbie jumped out and grabbed me. He punched me in the face; I remember my nose started bleeding. They called me a faggot again, other names. I tried to run away from them, but there were three, you know? They were football players." Joe's voice cracked.

"You don't have to do this," Kellie said softly, but deep down, she knew he did have to. He had to say it all out loud.

"They grabbed at my shorts. They pulled them down. I know I was crying, begging them to leave me alone. I was so scared, Kellie. Scott kicked me and I fell into a mud puddle, right on my bare ass. I struggled to get up. I was thinking I could run into the woods, maybe hide, anything. I heard glass break and could see Scott holding a beer bottle, the top broken off. All that jagged glass. And I thought I was going to pass out right there. I knew what he was planning to do with it."

"Oh, Joey." Kellie felt an overwhelming desire to gather him into her arms, tell him it would all be okay, but she was afraid to touch him. He was right on the edge.

"Just then I saw headlights coming up around the bend. It was my mom. The boys saw them, too, because they ran to the car and took off, burning rubber as they screamed out of there. And there it was, our Buick. My mom pulled up alongside me. I tried to stand, but my legs wouldn't let me, and I was curled up on the ground like a baby, wet and dirty. And as soon as she saw me, she got out of the car and ran to me. She helped me up and walked me to the car. I was afraid to get in, I was all muddy. My dad would be furious if I got the car dirty. She took off her London Fog and wrapped it around me, then put me in the car. I remember yelling at her. 'Why did you have to be late, Ma? Why?' I just cried all the way home. She kept saying she was sorry, she was crying, too. And then she sneaked me into the house and cleaned me up so my father wouldn't know." He took a long, ragged breath and bent forward at the waist, his head nearly resting on his knees. "And then I did the show the next night," he said. He raised himself up. Kellie saw his wet cheeks in the candlelight before he wiped away his tears.

"I never knew, Joe. I never knew anything about this. Suzanne never told me."

"She's a good secret keeper."

"How did you get through the rest of the year?"

"How? I don't know, I just did. I managed to avoid them somehow, and when I couldn't, they didn't do anything, not in front of the others. I had enough friends at school that I could always be surrounded by people. And then school was over."

"And then you left."

Joe poured an inch of scotch in each of their glasses. "Right after graduation. I knew I had to go. West Alton was suffocating. My father hated that I was gay. I'm not sure he hated *me*, but he hated that I wouldn't pretend to be straight for him. My grandparents gave me some money for graduation, and I bought a used car. A Dodge Diplomat." He laughed at the memory. "It was actually a good car! Took me across the country."

"I'm just in awe that you could do that at eighteen. Did you know anyone in California?"

"Nope. I got out here, had a little money, enough to rent a studio apartment. I found a job as a waiter pretty easily back then, and I started doing some modeling. Me and a thousand other pretty faces. But I didn't want to be an actor, I really did want to direct, I knew it even back then. But it took a while to learn the ropes, make my way. I had some good friends who helped me. I've never once regretted leaving."

They sat in comfortable silence for a few minutes. Tomorrow she and Suzanne would fly back to Rhode Island, Kellie thought. Joe had just shared what was probably his deepest secret with her. It would be too much tonight for her to tell Joe her own experience with Scott Hunter. Suzanne was the only one who knew, and, as Joe had said, she was a good secret keeper.

Finally she spoke. "How do you get through each day without that tearing you up inside? I mean, how do you put it aside and not let it dominate your life?"

"I don't know. I mean, it happened twenty-five years ago. Sometimes, it's as if it happened yesterday and I'm that teenager." He sat up straight again and faced her. "I ended, well, my partner, Paul, ended a five-year relationship recently. It was the best relationship I'd ever had. I thought we'd grow ancient together, really. And it hurts so much sometimes. It hurts more than what Scott Hunter and his band of thugs did to me."

"Sometimes I feel that the bad things in my life are what define me."

"How, Kellie?"

"Well, like my first marriage. I married a guy when I was in law school. Jonathan. He used to beat me up. The last time he hit me, he put me in the hospital. Why would I have married a guy like that?"

"You married a prick. You must have believed some part of him was good, though."

"I think maybe I was just grateful that someone was willing to marry me. I didn't stop to think about it much. I guess self-esteem finds its own level, like water. Today, though, I'd never put up with anyone hitting me. I'd rather be alone."

"How did you get away from him? You found the strength somehow."

"I got away because he broke my face, that's how. He was arrested and charged with domestic assault. When it happened, I was almost done with law school. This guy I worked for, Ed, he's a lawyer. He's still a friend, actually. He took care of me when Adam – my half-brother – killed my mom. That happened when I was in the hospital. Maybe Suzanne told you." Wow, she'd said it. That was a lot, and a lot to lay on Joe so late at night.

"She did tell me about that." Joe laid a hand over Kellie's. "I'm so sorry, Kellie."

"He stabbed her. He wanted money." She laughed at the absurdity. "She never had any money, we lived in a trailer. We were on food stamps. But he needed drugs, and money to buy them. And he killed her over it."

"And he's still in prison?"

Kellie nodded. "I'm sure he is; I don't have anything to do with him. He's not a part of my life."

"I can understand that." He rattled the ice in his glass. "So you had plastic surgery to fix your broken face. Kellie, you know you're beautiful, right?"

Kellie barked a short laugh again. "I should thank Jonathan for making me pretty." She was quiet, and stared out at the inky ocean. Now she turned her head back to Joe, one pretty face to another.

"Kellie, I think that by walking up to the past, a past that hurt me badly, I can put it away for good. I mean, I know this is armchair psychology. I practice it on myself all the time. It's why I'm going back to the reunion. To face Scott and Will and Robbie. God, I hope they show!" Joe threw his hands up. "Kellie, come with us, we'll have fun. I'm sure those guys are all fat and bald now."

Kellie smiled at him in the candlelight.

23

September 17 – 74 days to go

Amber and Tiffany, Cherry's best friends in high school, drove down from Exeter for a visit. Gwen prepared lunch, but had no desire to stay around.

"Neither one of them has come to visit you until now," she said, whisking lemon juice with olive oil and tarragon for the salad. "They're supposed to be your best friends."

"Tiffany works for her father, Gwen, and Amber, well, you know Amber." Her voice trailed off. Cherry wasn't really looking forward to this meeting, either. She knew her friends would be shocked by her appearance, and she'd have to try and put them at ease. Some people just didn't deal well with cancer, or any illness; she knew that. And her friends were vain, let's face it. As vain as Cherry used to be. They weren't going to know what to say when they saw her, so she'd have to carry the conversation. She wouldn't tell them how bad it was. As far as they knew, she'd had both breasts removed. They didn't need to know all the details.

"Okay, kiddo. I'm going to set up the table. It's air-conditioned in here, so everything will keep. You can eat whenever you want."

"Gwen, please stay." Cherry looked imploringly at her sister. "I know you don't want to, but I wish you would."

Gwen sighed. "I'm really afraid I won't be able to hold my tongue if one of them says something rude to you."

Cherry laughed. "You know them! They're going to be all, 'Oh my gawd, Cher, what the hell?' That's Amber." Gwen's face split into a wide grin at Cherry's imitation. "And this'll be Tiff: 'Can't you wear a wig or something instead of that scarf?' Am I right?"

Both of them dissolved into laughter. "All right, I'll stay," Gwen said. "But if it gets bad, don't blame me for pouring salad dressing on their heads."

The doorbell rang and both women froze. "Serious faces," Cherry whispered. "Roll me to the door." Gwen stepped behind her and gripped the chair's handles, then wheeled her sister to the front door. Cherry grasped the handle and pulled the door open, to see her girlfriends' faces drop to the ground.

"Come on in," she said in a bright voice as Gwen rolled her back. Amber was first, followed by Tiffany. Cherry noticed they'd both dressed up for the big event. Amber, still sporting a long curly perm and shiny pink lipstick, pressed her fingertips to her cheeks.

"Oh, Cher," she said, ignoring Cherry's outstretched arms. "I didn't know it was this bad."

Tiffany stepped from behind her, wearing tight black Bermuda shorts and white high-heeled sandals. Her legs were impossibly tan and she was thinner than ever. Well, Cherry thought, for once I'm as thin as you are, Tiff. "Oh my gawd, Cher," she said, and Cherry bit her tongue to keep from laughing.

"I feel a lot better than I look," Cherry said gamely. "Come on in, I'm not contagious!" Gwen wheeled her into the sunny kitchen, and right up to the table.

"Did you do all this?" Amber's mouth hadn't yet closed, but she did seem to be getting her bearings back. Somewhat.

"No, Gwen did it all," Cherry said. "You both remember Gwen, right? She lives with us now."

"Hey," Gwen said, and Cherry held her breath as the women surveyed each other. She was really glad Gwen had had her roots done yesterday; her hair looked great.

"Sit down! Tell me everything that's new." Cherry was determined to be upbeat.

"Cher, I am so sorry I haven't had the time to visit since you got sick. I spend more time every day driving the twins to soccer, to the pool club, to someone's house. Gawd, I never have a minute to myself," Amber said, shaking her head. She reached down into her purse and pulled out a hair clip. Cherry couldn't believe it.

"Is that…is that a banana clip?"

Amber grinned, nodding. She pulled her hair back from her head and secured it with the clip. If it weren't for the crinkles around her eyes and mouth, it could have been 1988 again. Amber looked exactly as she had in high school. Oh my gawd, thought Cherry.

"Look at all this food!" Tiffany exclaimed. "We can't eat all of this!" Tiffany actually looked frightened, as if Gwen might force-feed her.

"Just eat what you want, sweetie." Gwen widened her eyes so only Cherry could see.

"So, tell me what's going on with the reunion," Amber said. She took a spoonful of chicken salad and passed the bowl to Tiffany who inspected it, wrinkled her nose, and set it down without taking any. "Do you need me to help?"

Cherry knew Amber would be useless, so she ignored the question. If either Amber or Tiffany had wanted to help, they'd have stepped up by now. No, Cherry would handle it. With Gwen, who wasn't even in the class of 1988. The Weiss sisters would take care of everything.

"I have a lot of responses already. I got both of your checks, thanks. The place looks good, doesn't it, Gwen?" She turned her face to Gwen, who nodded and continued to busy herself with eating and refilling glasses of iced tea.

"We checked it out and it's the perfect size. So," she continued, setting down her fork, "out of a hundred classmates, I think we'll have about seventy-five, including spouses and dates."

"Wow, that's awesome." Tiffany picked up a lettuce leaf between her fingers and nibbled on it, like a five-year-old would do. Cherry wondered if she did the same thing at home, where she still lived with her parents. Maybe her mother still cut her meat for her. "Tell us who's coming."

Cherry rattled off some names and her friends nodded along in recognition. When she mentioned Joe Traversa, Amber squealed. "He's coming? From Hollywood?"

Cherry shrugged. "Looks that way. And Suzanne Fitch, remember her?"

Amber frowned and Tiffany scrunched up her face. "What did she look like?" Amber asked.

"Normal. Just a regular, normal girl, I guess." Cherry's reply drew more scrunching. They were trying to remember, Cherry thought. I'd better not mention Kellie Blunt.

"Anyway, I'm really excited that Joe's coming. He's the most famous person to graduate from West Alton High." Cherry glanced at Gwen. Tiffany had eaten lettuce and a cherry tomato. Amber had at least eaten some of the chicken salad. "You guys want coffee? I have blueberry cake." The girls exchanged a worried glance. "What?" Cherry looked from one to the other.

"Well, we don't do carbs," Amber said.

"Or sugar," Tiffany added.

Cherry raised her eyebrows and would not meet the gaze she knew was being leveled at her from Gwen at the sink. "How about just coffee then?"

*

October 2 – 59 days to go

Scott called Molly, but she wouldn't return his phone calls. He didn't get it; she was really into him last month. He left a couple of messages for her, but dammit, he wasn't going to beg. He knew Liz would be around, but he had to admit, time spent with a young girl like Molly, all plump and round and squishy, was fun. Liz was all dried up and smelled like smoke. He sat on his deck and stared at her empty parking space. He hadn't seen the white car there for a couple of weeks now, and he wondered if she'd moved out.

He called Will and they met up at the sports bar in town, next to the library.

"Hey bro, what's going on?" Will landed on the barstool next to Scott.

"Nothing," Scott said sulkily. He picked at the label on his beer bottle.

"Someone's not gettin' laid," Will teased, until he caught Scott's dark look and raised two fingers to the bartender. "Two more of these," he said, then turned back to Scott. "So what's up?"

"I called Molly a coupla times. She won't call me back. I think she mighta moved away."

"*What?* I thought she was just an easy lay, man. You interested in her? What is she, like twenty?"

Scott shrugged. "Twenty-four, I don't know. Liz bores the hell out of me these days. She's too fuckin' old, man. And she smells like an ashtray." He stared up at the flat screen television mounted above the bar. The six o'clock news was on with closed-captioning. He pointed up to the television with his chin. "What the hell is this?"

Will followed his gaze, then lowered his voice to a conspiratorial whisper. "Man, I've been telling you. Watch your back. See that guy? He's doing a series on disability pensions. Be careful, brother."

Scott let out a low whistle. "Shit, man. What is that, undercover stuff?" They both watched a grainy film showing a man in a gym, lifting weights.

"Hey, that could be Bobby, man. Doesn't that look like Bobby?"

Scott stared at the screen, but the news had moved on to footage of an ethnic festival in the city. "Sheesh. Last thing I need is to show up on TV," he said.

"No shit. Watch. Your. Back. Leave the bike in our shed. I'm serious. You're supposed to be permanently disabled. Don't let them catch you."

"Yeah." Scott signaled for two more beers and looked around the bar.

"Call Liz," said Will. "Forget the fat girl."

"She was more fun."

"Stick with what you know, brother."

*

Kellie knew that Jeff Braun appreciated her work, even if he didn't say so often. She was detailed-oriented and stayed until the assignment was done. The investigative team had completed all their undercover filming by Labor Day weekend, when she was in California with Suzanne and Joe, and she had categorized it. The team had footage for ten different people – eight men, two women – who were collecting disability pensions. The first piece aired the previous Tuesday, and would be rerun twice during the week.

Kellie had categorized eight of the videos and pulled up the ninth, marked "Hunter." She stopped, and her stomach clenched at the name. There were plenty of Hunters in this state, she thought, but inwardly, she already knew. It was Scott Hunter. She loaded the video and watched. Scott Hunter jumping on a motorcycle, riding away. Scott Hunter returning, with a young blonde on the back. Jumping off, helping her off. Running up a flight of outside stairs to a second-level apartment. Oh my God, running into the ocean, with the girl on his back. Playing in the waves. Hoisting her above his head, dropping her into the water. This was good footage. Kellie checked the information sheet. Back injury. Ha. He'd worked for the West Alton Fire Department and was collecting upwards of forty thousand a year, tax free. Not for long, Scott Hunter. So this is what retribution looks like, Kellie said to herself. She thought she'd be gleeful about it, but she wasn't.

Jeff Braun appeared in her doorway. "We got some good feedback on the series so far," he said. He leaned against the door frame, hands in his pockets, a crooked grin on his face.

Kellie looked up and waved him in. "This one, this Scott Hunter," she said evenly. "This might be the best one. I'd recommend ending the series with him. When is the last one supposed to air?"

Jeff peered at a calendar on her wall. "Elizabeth said she wants one every week, you know, to build anticipation. And we end in November, during sweeps. So," he tapped numbers on the page, then flipped to the next month, "we'll finish at the end of November." He glanced back at Kellie.

Perfect, she thought. "Great. This guy should be the last one."

"We never would have had such good film if it wasn't for the girlfriend. You saw the blonde? She clued us in on his every move. But anyway, however you want to place these is fine with me. I'm leaving all of that stuff up to you." Jeff shuffled his feet. "Um, if you ever wanted to grab dinner or something…"

Oh. "Sure," she said, drawing out the word. Was he asking her out? "As colleagues, right? I'm, well, I'm with someone, but sure, we could get a bite sometime."

His face reddened and she realized he had, indeed, asked her out on a date, in his awkward, self-conscious way.

"Absolutely, as colleagues," he said, waving his hand. "I should get back to work. See you, Kellie."

"See you, Jeff."

Kellie watched him leave. Well, she never talked about Bill, so how was he to know? Still, she wasn't interested in anyone else, even if it felt as though her relationship with Bill was stuck in neutral. They had weekends, and he usually stayed over on Saturday night, but there wasn't much more to say about it. It hadn't really grown. Was it enough? Hard to know, Kellie thought. She was so busy right now that there wouldn't be time to see him during the week, and she'd told him that when the project began. He seemed to understand, and Kellie knew he was busy, too. Maybe once this was done, they'd be able to move forward.

Meanwhile, she wondered if Jeff might be interested in Camille. She'd have to work that in somehow. Maybe a double date. She'd ask Bill first.

24

November 1 – 29 days to go

Cherry awoke with a renewed sense of energy and purpose. The reunion was four weeks away and she was totally focused on it. For the past month, she'd eaten nothing but fresh fruits and vegetables, grass-fed beef, free-range chicken. No sugar, no dairy, no processed foods. She believed she'd be in great shape by then. Her hair was growing back, very gray, she noticed with a grin, so she kept the wig. She was used to it now. And after the surgery to remove the lymph nodes, her doctor had nothing but encouraging reports.

And Nita was engaged! Cherry would admit now that she'd been worried, concerned that Bud would seek solace and comfort in his employee's arms, but he'd come home the other night and announced that she'd be leaving in three weeks. Cherry was so happy, she asked Gwen to help her make a chocolate cake for Bud. He was looking for someone new to manage the restaurant, so he could spend more time at home, in spite of her protestations that she was fine. Nick was on the soccer team and had joined the debate club. Cherry smiled at the thought of her beautiful boy. Athletic and smart, she reminded herself. And growing up so fast. His phone buzzed constantly with calls and texts, something Cherry didn't ask him about, as much as she wanted to know. There were just some things a boy didn't tell his mother. She wondered if he'd had sex yet and reminded Bud to talk with Nick again about respect and protection. He wouldn't want to hear it from his mother.

Nick was gorgeous and exotic, like Bud, and Cherry understood why girls were drawn to him. That smile, the whitest teeth, black eyes, shiny black hair. Her boy was a chick magnet, thought Cherry. Whoever Nick chooses will be okay, she said to herself. I will not be a monster-in-law. Her eyes misted as she realized she was thinking so far ahead, years into the future. *Will I even still be here?* Cancer can always come back. Be positive, she reminded herself.

She reviewed the RSVP list, checking it against the roster of classmates. Scott Hunter and his gang. Cherry frowned. She still hadn't heard back from Kellie Blunt, although she had responses and payments from her friend Suzanne and from Joe Traversa. Cherry imagined Kellie wouldn't want to attend. And yet, she really wanted Kellie to be there. She checked her list again and telephoned Suzanne Fitch.

"Suzanne, hi, it's Cherry Weiss. I'm wondering if you wouldn't mind giving me a number where I could reach Kellie. I really wanted to speak with her about the reunion."

"Oh. Has she contacted you? I don't know if she decided about it."

"You said she might be going, but I haven't heard from her, and I'd really like to call her."

"Um, okay. Well, I have her number at work. Hold on."

Cherry waited until Suzanne recited the number, then she thanked her and dialed the number. She was surprised when a voice answered. "Channel 8, good morning."

So Kellie worked at the television station in Providence. Cherry nodded, impressed.

"Kellie Campbell, please," she said, remembering the name change.

"I'll connect you," a woman said. Cherry's heart pounded and she felt a dizziness rise from her gut. She had no idea how Kellie would react. High school was a long time ago.

"This is Kellie Campbell." Cherry started to speak before she realized it was Kellie's voice mail. She listened to the rest of the recording. At the tone, she started speaking.

"Kellie, this is Cherry Weiss. From high school. I just wanted to reach out to you. Um, I hope you'll come to the reunion next month. I'd really like to see you." She hesitated. "Twenty-five years is a long time. And, well, I hope you'll come." She left her telephone number and hung up, and realized she was breathing hard. Why was that so difficult? Cherry knew why.

Kellie Blunt was the girl no one bothered with. The weird girl, whose clothes were out of fashion, who lived in a trailer and didn't gossip with all the other girls. Whose hair wasn't long and curly, tied with ribbons. Cherry knew that, while she didn't go out of her way to be mean to Kellie, like some girls did, she was guilty through her complacency. She'd stand with Amber and Tiffany and Deirdre and listen to them disparage Kellie. And she never defended her. Of course not, she wouldn't risk being ostracized herself.

The telephone rang and Cherry jumped. Could it be Kellie already? She grabbed the receiver. "Hello?"

"Cherry, this is Kellie Campbell. Kellie Blunt. I got your message."

Cherry steadied herself. "Hi, Kellie. Thanks so much for calling me back."

"Wow, are there so few people attending the reunion that you're calling everyone?" That laugh, like sunlight dancing over the waves. Cherry had never heard Kellie's laugh. It was pretty, she thought.

"No, actually, I called because I hadn't heard back from you and I was hoping you'd attend. I'd have liked to see you again."

"Why?" The question hung in the air for seconds as Cherry groped for a reply.

"Because. Because I should have made more of an effort to know you. Because time goes by…" Cherry's voice caught and she struggled to keep her tone even. "I'm just reminiscing, I guess, getting emotional." Tears spilled from her eyes. "Your friends are coming. Suzanne Fitch. Even Joe Traversa, all the way from Hollywood."

"I know," said Kellie softly. "Cherry, in your invitation, you asked people to submit their most memorable moment from high school."

"Yes." Cherry took a breath. "Silly idea."

"No, it was a good idea. I hope you've received some interesting memories."

Cherry laughed quietly. "Yes, some. Kellie? If you decide not to attend the reunion, would you come to my house for lunch? I'd really like to see you." She held her breath.

"That's very kind." And after a moment, Kellie added, "Sure, I'd love to see you, too."

"Are you free tomorrow?" Cherry tried to keep the desperation out of her voice.

"Okay. Sure. I could come tomorrow." Jeff wouldn't need her this weekend.

"Great! That would be great." Cherry recited her address to Kellie, repeated her phone number, and asked if she liked Indian food. "My husband runs an Indian restaurant here in town."

"That sounds terrific. Thanks for the invitation. I'll see you on Saturday."

Cherry hung up and gulped air. She was covered in sweat. "Gwen!" she shouted. "Come here, quick!"

*

Kellie finished work and packed up her files, then placed everything in a locked cabinet and pocketed the key. Her office door didn't have a lock, but when she began the project, she'd told Jeff that she'd have to have a locked storage area for the files, as they contained confidential information that couldn't be seen by anyone else.

If she was meeting Cherry Weiss in Falmouth for lunch on Saturday, she wasn't sure Saturday night would work for a double date. She dialed Bill's number as she walked out of the office. Once she'd told him of her lunch plans, she mentioned her idea about getting Jeff and Camille together.

"Are you playing matchmaker now, Kellie?" he asked, and she knew he was smiling.

"I just think they would get along well. They know each other casually from working here together, but they're in different areas of the station. It makes it a little easier to be with us, don't you think?"

"And the three of you are going to talk shop all evening?"

"Gee, I hope not!" Kellie laughed. "Let me see if they're open to it and I'll call you back."

She hung up and crossed over the bridge, past the parking lot where Vic, the attendant, called out, "Hey, beautiful, when are you going to let me take you out to dinner?" Kellie grinned at him and called back, "When you're no longer married, Vic!"

He shrugged and held out his hands, palms up, saying, "Details, sweetheart, details." She waved and walked away, cutting through streets as she made her way toward her loft. This part of Providence cleared out early, as soon as office hours ended, and before the bars filled up.

A homeless man stepped out from a darkened doorway and startled her. As she jumped back, he grinned, showing rotten teeth. He held a bottle half-filled with a brownish liquid.

"Didn't mean to startle you, miss." He set the bottle on the sidewalk. "Any spare change?"

She dug in her pocket and handed him a ten-dollar bill. He looked down at the bill, then back up at her, puzzled.

His voice was calm, quiet. "Thank you kindly, miss," he said.

"What's your name?" She didn't back away, in spite of the man's stench.

"Everybody calls me Shorty, miss."

She knew that ten dollars wouldn't help him much. It wouldn't get him a shower, or a bed, or new clothes. He could get a meal at the fast-food place. She gave him money because she'd walked by homeless men every day, the few in the city who'd become familiar to her as she walked to and from work, and she'd never given money to any of them before. She gave him money because she didn't know what else to do. But she could at least call this man by his name.

"Shorty, see if you can get something to eat, okay?"

"Okay."

"And stay safe." She turned to walk away.

"Bless you, miss," he called after her.

25

November 1 – 29 days to go

Back inside her fortress, Kellie shed her bags and clothes. She figured she'd better call Jeff first, since she was pretty sure Camille would be game for meeting just about anyone.

"Jeff, it's me, Kellie."

"Kellie! Wow, a call at home. I'm flattered." He chuckled into the phone and Kellie could have sworn his voice was deeper.

"Don't be, I'm calling with a proposition." She winced; that came out wrong.

"I'm listening," he said slowly.

"Do you know Camille Rohr at work? Dark hair, big smile?"

Silence. "Yeah, I know who she is. Why?"

"Well, I was just thinking you two might enjoy each other's company. Bill and I wanted the two of you to join us tomorrow evening. Nothing fancy, just pizza and beer at that place by the marina. Very casual, Jeff."

"You're setting me up, Kellie. Does Camille think this is a date?"

Kellie paced the floor and cursed silently. "I haven't even called her yet, Jeff. I wanted to ask you first. It's not a date, really. If there's no chemistry, you don't have to worry; it's just a few friends getting together. Please say yes."

"So I can sit with you and your boyfriend? Kellie, I don't know."

"And you won't know unless you spend some time with her. Look, I've been on enough blind dates to know they can be awkward. But it would be a lot easier if we all went together. And I promise you, I will not let her think that this is a date – just asking you along because we work together now. Okay?"

She listened to him exhale on the other end. Finally he spoke. "Okay. I don't want to hurt her feelings. I've seen her around the office, Kellie. She's, well, she's not really my type, physically."

Kellie squeezed her eyes shut. They were all the same. She controlled her voice and spoke slowly. "Okay. So just consider it meeting a colleague, nothing more. Tomorrow at seven at Luigi's."

"Yep. Okay. I'm doing this for you." He clicked off.

Kellie poured a glass of wine before she dialed Camille's number. It took her three times to convey, and underscore, the fact that it wasn't a blind date. "I wanted you to meet Bill for a long time, and I work with Jeff now."

"But it really *is* a blind date, isn't it?" She giggled nervously.

"Nope, it's really not. Just some colleagues getting together. Don't think of it as anything more than that, Camille. I don't want you to be disappointed."

"I know. Jeff knows who I am, and I'm sure I'm not the kind of girl he'd be interested in anyway. Maybe if he weighed three hundred pounds or something."

"You know what, Camille? Think of it as coming out with Bill and me, and Jeff just happens to show up. I'm not even sure he's good enough for you." She meant it; stupid Jeff. The girls weren't beating a path to *his* door.

"Thanks, Kellie," she said softly. "I'll be there."

*

November 2 – 28 days to go

Joe ran out of excuses and picked up the phone to call his father. He'd done twenty minutes of calming exercises first, but he felt his blood pressure rise even as he dialed the number.

"Traversa." Joe almost laughed out loud at his father's habit of answering a call.

"Hey, Dad. Just calling to see how you're doing." Just tell me you're fine, Joe thought, so I can make this quick.

"My electric bill went up twelve bucks. And I used less. This morning I was almost run over by a twerp in a hot rod who had that idiotic rap music turned up so loud he couldn't hear me yelling at him. Probably on drugs, too."

"Well, I'm glad you weren't hit, Dad." Deep breath, exhale.

"And the fuckin' fags around here. What the hell, maybe California's sendin' them all to live here. Them and the Spanish. I never even hear English anymore. Buncha animals."

Choose your words, Joe could hear his mother saying calmly.

"They're people, Dad, not animals." He touched the framed photograph of him and Paul, the one he rescued from his bottom drawer last week and placed back on his desk.

"You chose that life, why, I'll never know," the old man muttered.

"You think this is a choice, Dad?" He ran a finger over the glass, over their smiling faces.

"Of course it's a choice," his father shouted back. "You coulda settled down with a nice girl, had a family, made us all happy."

"Made who happy, Dad? You?"

"You broke your mother's heart. Ah, fuck it."

Joe counted silently to ten, then said, "Goodbye, Dad." He hung up and threw the photograph across the room, where it smashed into the wall and fell to the floor in pieces.

*

Kellie stopped at the florist's for a bouquet. She waited while he picked orange and yellow dahlias, copper Echinacea, and green gladiolus and tied them together with brown ribbon, then wrapped everything in paper and presented the finished bouquet to her.

"Perfect, thanks," she said. She drove to Falmouth, an hour and twenty minutes away, and used her GPS to find Cherry's modern house in Sippewissett, close to Woods Hole. She pulled into the circular driveway and shut off the engine, then bowed her head for a moment before taking the bouquet and walking to the front door. Two white Adirondack chairs sat on the porch in the shade, with a basket of cheery yellow chrysanthemums in a basket on a table.

The woman who opened the door looked a little like Cherry Weiss, but it had been twenty-five years, and well, everyone ages, right?

"Cherry."

"No, I'm Gwen, Cherry's sister. You must be Kellie. Come on in." The woman pulled the front door open and Kellie stepped into a house that could be featured in a magazine. The house was filled with natural light, even though some of the trees still had their leaves. Gwen led her to the back of the house, through an immense, immaculate kitchen, to a small woman sitting in a wheelchair. Kellie's breath caught in her throat.

The woman turned around and grinned. "Kellie? Well, aren't you beautiful!"

Kellie swallowed hard and licked her lips. This? This is Cherry Weiss? She was a skeleton. A grinning skeleton who extended a hand on an arm that was like a piece of kindling.

Kellie regained her composure and took Cherry's bony hand in hers. "Hi, Cherry. It's good to see you."

"Sit down, please. I'm sorry my appearance is so shocking."

"No, no…"

Cherry leveled a gaze at her. "I know it is. I'm apologizing because it was hard to say it over the phone. I have cancer. I'm still fighting, and I expect to be at the reunion at the end of the month, but, oh, damn this cancer!" Her laugh was dry and hoarse.

"I'm really sorry." Kellie leaned toward her.

Cherry waved a hand in her general direction. "Come on, Gwen fixed a nice lunch for us. I didn't know what you liked, but when I mentioned Indian food, you didn't freak out." She stared at Kellie with hollow eyes. Kellie tried hard to picture the cheerleader with the shiny dark hair, the easy laugh. The group of them standing near the lockers, laughing. At her.

Kellie took a seat at the table and Gwen wheeled Cherry to sit on her right. Kellie saw a yearbook lying on the table. She pointed. "Our yearbook?"

Cherry nodded and picked it up. "Oh, it's heavy," she groaned, sliding it instead between them. "When I was making the list to contact everyone about the reunion, I missed you, because you're not in here." She turned her head to look at Kellie.

"No." Kellie blinked hard at the rush of memory. "I didn't have a picture taken."

"You've had some work done, though." It was a simple statement, not an accusation. Kellie looked at Cherry and smiled.

"Let's call it involuntary work done. My first husband broke my face." She saw Cherry's eyes widen.

"I'm sorry," she whispered. Kellie nodded.

"It's a better face, though, isn't it?" She looked into Cherry's eyes until Cherry nodded and looked away, blinking rapidly.

Gwen placed a bowl of salad and a platter of tandoori chicken on the table. "Cherry's husband Bud made this," she said. "And here's some bread."

Cherry asked, "Do you eat bread?"

"I love bread!" Kellie replied with a laugh. "I probably shouldn't, but I do love my carbs."

Cherry took Kellie's hand and squeezed it.

*

After lunch, Cherry and Kellie sat in the sunroom, enjoying the afternoon light and view of Buzzards Bay. Kellie glanced at her watch.

"Do you have to leave already?" Cherry asked.

"No, not yet." Kellie cleared her throat and shifted in her chair. "Cherry, you had asked all of us to submit a memory to you, something memorable from senior year."

"Yes," Cherry said, bowing her head. "But I wanted to say something to you first. Kellie, I know it was high school, but I could have been a better person to you. I could have been nicer."

Kellie saw Cherry's eyes fill up, so she spoke quickly. "It was high school. We were all young. And you were never mean to me."

"My friends were, though. And I didn't do anything to defend you. I know they made fun of you, for your clothes, your hair."

"My nose, my teeth," Kellie added. "It was a long time ago. It's okay. Those were your friends, and there's a lot of pressure to get along, to do what the others do. If you had stuck up for me then, you would have lost your friends." Self-preservation. Everyone does it. "I am going to come to the reunion, Cherry. I'll give you a check before I leave."

Cherry touched her palms together. Kellie figured clapping expended too much energy, and Cherry looked so tired.

"I'm so happy. I told you Joe Traversa is coming, right?"

Kellie smiled, remembering the evening in Malibu. She thought about the courage it took for him to tell her what had happened to him.

"Cherry, I want to tell you what happened to me in high school. It's probably one of the only things I remember about that time, outside of the tie-dyed clothes my mother made me wear, or the fact that we couldn't afford braces for my teeth. And I want to tell you because it's important for me to share this with someone. To not keep it buried any longer."

Cherry waited, small in her wheelchair, bony hands clasped together in her lap.

"It was a few days before graduation and we'd been dismissed early from school. My half-brother Adam had a recital or something at the middle school, so my mother had gone up there to see him. I was walking home, and because we lived at the edge of the big Watson farm, I took the shortcut that I knew well. It was a worn path, not so much a road, but we called it Orchard Lane. It was wide enough for one car. There were little spots to pull off the road where the kids could park their cars and they'd be mostly hidden from anyone who happened to use the shortcut, too. Suzanne told me some of the kids would drive there at night to make out in the woods.

"I remember the trees made a canopy overhead and everything was green and thick and lush. The gypsy moth nests were everywhere in the trees, masses of white and gray netting that held fat caterpillars. I remember looking up at the trees and hoping the caterpillars wouldn't drop out of them and land on me. I loved the quiet and the solitude and the fact that we were graduating in only a couple of days. I'd received a full scholarship to attend

Northwestern, and my guidance counselor had found a place for me to live. I was really looking forward to everything." Kellie took a sip of water and swallowed.

"About a half-mile from home, I heard a car behind me, so I stepped over to the side to let it pass. It was Scott Hunter. He had a Mustang, and he stopped ahead of me. I saw his arm hanging out the car window, and he had a bottle of beer in his hand. I turned to keep walking and he called to me to stop. I knew who he was; I knew he played on the football team. So I walked over to the driver's side. He offered me a beer, but I refused. He turned off the ignition and got out of the car. He looked me up and down, and asked me why I was walking down a deserted path. I told him I was on my way home. 'C'mere,' he said, slurring the two words together. I didn't want to go over to him, but I was nervous that he'd get mad. I didn't want to get Scott Hunter mad. I saw him one time on the football field and he just plowed into a guy on the other team."

Kellie closed her eyes as she remembered the details. She could picture the day in her mind, early June, a day bursting with life. She opened her eyes and looked at Cherry, who stared at her in rapt attention.

"He somehow walked me around to the other side of the car, the side where the woods were. We were hidden because there was so much growth, so much green. If someone had come down the path, they would have seen an abandoned car. 'How come you never talk to me?' he asked. He leaned back against his car and drank his beer. I couldn't find any words to speak. I remember just standing there, about a foot away from him, backed up to the woods. He looked me up and down and started laughing. 'Shit, you really are ugly,' he said."

Kellie glanced at Cherry just then, saw her wince.

"He opened the back door of his car and pulled out another bottle of beer. He held it out to me, and again I shook my head no. Then he pushed me inside the car. I kind of fell forward, so my face was on the back seat. It smelled like beer and vomit, and I remember thinking I might be sick, and how mad he'd be at me if I threw up in his car. I felt him pull at my long skirt, laughing. He threw a bottle on the ground and it broke, and I was paralyzed with fear. I knew he was going to rape me, I just knew. And I was afraid to move. I mean, I knew I should fight back, or at least struggle, but I was frozen. I couldn't move."

Kellie shook her head. She'd come this far, she had to finish the story. Cherry was waiting. *Tell it*, a voice inside her said, *let this secret out.*

"I felt him push against me, like he was going to push into me. I know I was crying. Then he grabbed my shirt and pulled me out of the car. He threw me on the ground and said, 'You're even too ugly from behind. I can't stand to look at you.' He laughed and shut the car door. I was sitting on the broken bottle. My palm had a piece of glass in it and I was bleeding. And he slipped into the driver's seat, started the car, and took off down the road."

Cherry had a hand covering her mouth. Tears streamed from her eyes.

"I ran home. No one was there. I picked the glass from my hand and used some alcohol on it. Then I took a bath. I knew I had cuts on my behind, but I didn't want my mother to know. She had her hands full with Adam." Kellie closed her eyes again and tried to dismiss any mental images of Adam and her mother.

"You were supposed to speak at our graduation. Weren't you like the number two student?" Cherry wiped at her eyes.

Kellie nodded. "Salutatorian, yes. I didn't go to graduation. They mailed my diploma to me. I just stayed in bed and told my mother I was sick. She didn't ask any questions. Two weeks later I moved to Chicago for school."

"Oh, Kellie." Cherry wiped again at her eyes. "I don't know what to say. Sorry isn't nearly enough. But I'm so, so sorry any of this happened to you."

Kellie stood up and walked to the window. There was a boat on the water, just a small boat with no sail, bobbing on the waves. She turned back to Cherry.

"I married a rotten guy when I was in law school. I probably didn't think I was worth anyone good and decent." She waved a hand in front of her face. "After he beat me up and put me in the hospital, I realized I had to leave him. Surgeons fixed my face, but I needed to heal the rest of me. I needed to value myself."

Kellie walked over to Cherry's wheelchair and crouched next to it. She took Cherry's hands in hers. "I'm glad you asked me here today. You're a good person, Cherry. And I'll see you next month." She pulled a folded check from her purse. "Thank you for lunch. Thank Gwen, too, please."

"I wish you didn't have to go," Cherry said.

Kellie smiled. "I'll see you soon," she said, then bent to kiss Cherry's cheek, surprising even herself. She let herself out the door.

26

November 29 – 1 day to go

Joe arrived in Mystic on Friday, the day before the reunion. Kellie drove down after a shortened day at work, thanks to Jeff Braun. He was a happy man these days. The station's ratings were great, thanks to the investigative pieces that ran each week, and there was buzz about him receiving a New England Emmy nod. Camille was making him happy these days, too. That double date, that wasn't really a double date, turned out to be pretty magical after all, at least for Camille and Jeff.

The following day, nearly four weeks ago now, Bill told her the firm was transferring him to Philadelphia.

"What?" Kellie almost lost her balance. She sat down hard.

"They want me to head up a new satellite office there." He fidgeted. He pushed his eggs around on his plate. He sipped coffee. But he didn't say anything more.

"I see. Well, that's good news for you, isn't it?"

"Kellie. It would be great news if you'd come with me." He reached for her hand, but she saw it coming and hid hers under the table. "I can't say no to this offer."

She shook her head. "Of course you can't! This is a wonderful opportunity for you. But my job is here."

"Philly's not that far away, you know. We've only been able to see each other on the weekends anyway. Maybe we could still see each other on the weekends. You take the train down, I drive up."

Kellie knew that wouldn't work, not for long. "Sure. When you do leave?"

"Next week."

"So soon."

"I hope you'll tell me all about your reunion." He tried to smile. Kellie tried, too, and wondered if her eyes reflected as much sadness as his did.

He still called her, every other day or so. Kellie knew that, after a few weeks, maybe after the holidays, he'd call less often, then never. Next month, she'd go back to working for Elizabeth.

"It's my high school reunion tomorrow night," Kellie said to Jeff as she switched her heels for flats.

"How many years?" Jeff leaned in the doorway, hands in his pockets as usual. Kellie noticed he'd put on weight, most likely due to Camille's cooking. He looked healthier.

"Twenty-five," she said, shaking her head. "Hard to believe."

"I have a thirtieth next summer. How the heck does time go by so fast?"

"Less of it to waste away, I suppose," she said. "I'll see you on Monday." She stopped in the hallway. "The last segment is airing tomorrow night, right?"

He nodded. "Yeah. Elizabeth really didn't want to air it on a Saturday night, but I told her there was so much anticipation with these stories, and people recorded shows now anyway, so she agreed. Hey, why were you so adamant that this one be shown tomorrow night?"

Kellie shrugged. "Just figured it was time, you know, holiday weekend. The station's been teasing it all week."

She patted his shoulder on her way out. "Tell Camille I'll call her for lunch soon."

Kellie had driven to work that morning, parking in the underground garage. She pulled a ticket from her coat pocket and handed it to the young man, who glanced at it, and jogged up to the next level. In a minute, she heard her car's engine as he drove it down and parked right in front of her. She handed the kid some money and buckled herself in. It was only four o'clock but already dusky. They were just weeks away from the shortest day of the year. Kellie turned on her headlights and headed out to the highway.

She and Suzanne had booked a room at the same hotel where Joe was staying. For Friday and Saturday. And Joe had a car for Saturday night, so no one would have to worry about driving all the way back from the reunion. She spotted Suzanne's car in the parking lot and pulled in next to it. They'd planned a simple dinner at the Mystic Marina that evening, and Kellie wanted a chance to change her clothes and freshen up.

She knocked on the door of the room number Suzanne had given her, and Joe opened the door.

"Oh, it's good to see you!" He grabbed her in a tight embrace, lifting her off her feet, and Kellie waved at Suzanne over his shoulder.

When he set her down, she laid her hand against his face. "You look good. They're all going to fall at your feet tomorrow night."

He grabbed his side, and, seeing the worried look on Kellie's face, explained. "The sword of panic."

"Stop," Suzanne said from the sofa. She lifted a glass of golden wine. "Come have a drink, Kell."

"Just let me wash up," Kellie said. When she returned, dressed as casually as her friends, she lifted her glass of wine. "What should we drink to?"

"To being young forever," said Joe. Kellie and Suzanne shot him looks and his face crinkled with laughter.

"To friendship, tested and true," Suzanne ventured. She drank, oblivious to whether her toast was acceptable.

"To the occasional glance back, and the focus on what's ahead," Kellie said. She toasted Suzanne, then Joe. "And here's to tomorrow night – may it be memorable." She smiled into her wine before sipping from the glass.

*

November 30

The following evening, the three of them climbed into a giant black Suburban.

"This thing is a gasoline pig," Suzanne complained as she stepped into the vehicle.

"Try not to think about it for one night, okay, sweetie?" Joe had his hand on the small of her back. He turned to help Kellie climb in.

"Thanks for doing this," she said, sliding in next to Suzanne.

"No one wants to have to drive to Quonset and back tonight," he said. He shut the door and the driver took off.

"We could pick up a few more people," Suzanne murmured, using her head to point to the additional row of seats behind them. "But this is really nice. Thanks, Joey. We're going to arrive in style."

"So you let Cherry know you'd be here tonight?" Joe said to Kellie.

She nodded. "I actually went to visit her a few weeks ago." At Joe's raised eyebrows, she added, "Suzanne knew. It was a nice visit." She looked down at her lap. "She's not well, you know. Cancer. It's taken a lot out of her. But she was very nice. I think that with death staring her down, she wanted to mend some fences before it was too late."

"It's always worth it to try. What did you two talk about?" Joe asked.

Kellie lifted one shoulder. "She apologized for being part of a group of mean girls." Now she lifted both shoulders and let them down. "It's all in the past, but I know it was important for her to say it." She smiled at her friends. "I'm actually fine about tonight."

"Well, you look fabulous," Joe said. "Both of you do."

"Oh, get over it, Joey. You're going to walk in that place and light up the entire room. As usual." Suzanne gave him a playful push.

*

Kellie was right, Joe thought. Cancer had taken its toll on Cherry Weiss. She was no longer the bouncy, sparkly cheerleader. Here she was, breakably thin in a wheelchair, wearing a fashionable but obvious wig. Yet that smile was still there, and Joe's heart swelled when he saw her.

He let the girls walk in ahead of him and noticed that no one really paid them much attention as they leaned over the long table and found name tags. He saw Suzanne clip hers to her neckline, and he watched as Kellie slipped hers into her purse. She's going incognito, he thought. Bravo, Kellie.

"Oh my gawd!" he heard someone scream and realized it was directed at him. He peered at the source of the commotion and concentrated. Who the heck was she? He tried to read her name badge but she came at him fast. "Joey Traversa! Oh my gawd!"

The mystery woman hugged him hard, and he looked over her shoulder at Suzanne, who winked and waved as she walked into the main dining room.

"Hey!" he said, pulling away. *Tiffany Bullock. Oh my gawd, indeed.* "Tiffany, look at you! Do you age at all?" He poured it on as the women started to swarm around him, as if he were made of sugar. Or money. Well...

"Are you making a new movie?" "Do you know anyone famous?" "Who do you know?" "Joe, I saw you on television, accepting the Oscar." "You're so handsome!" And he heard one of them mutter, "What a waste." He grinned through it all.

*

Scott Hunter perched on a stool at the bar, eying everyone who entered the lobby. He turned to Will. "Some of them got really fat," he sneered, lifting the bottle of Heineken to his lips. "At least we still have our hair," he added with a laugh. He drank from the bottle and set it down. Every now and then someone would walk up to the bar and order. Scott and Will sat at the opposite end, where they could conduct their own kind of surveillance on the attendees.

Two women walked in and made their way over to the table of name badges. He elbowed Will. "Who are those two?"

Will squinted. "The blonde looks familiar. She's not as pretty as the other one." He watched as they picked up badges and walked into the main dining room. "Dunno." Will let his fingers play over the sweating glass in front of him and pouted.

"Hey, bro, get over it, willya? We're here for a party. Where the hell is Robbie, anyway?"

Will looked around and shrugged. "He'll be here. And you don't understand. Ellen gave me hell about coming here without her."

Scott turned to face his friend. "What business does she have comin' to your frickin' high school reunion, huh? She doesn't know anyone here except me. And she don't like me. Any more than I like her." Then he thought about Ellen, dancing around the house in her underwear, and kind of wished she'd come with Will.

"She's my wife, idiot. She says we should do things together. Plus, I don't think she thinks you're a very good influence."

Scott roared. "Ha! Good one, bro. Never have been, and she knew it from the day she met me. Bad to the bone," he sang, pointing at his chest.

Kellie walked up to the bar and was directly in Scott's line of vision. She ordered a glass of wine and waited. She'd seen him at the bar before he noticed her. She wondered if he'd remember their encounter in the Tex-Mex restaurant this past summer.

"Well, hello," she heard him say as he sidled up on her left. "I know it's been twenty-five years, but I'm not sure I know you. You look familiar, though."

She turned halfway to face him and looked down at his badge. "Scott Hunter," she said with no inflection in her voice.

"And where's your name badge? Oh, please don't tell me you're somebody's wife." He ran a hand through his hair and put a twenty-dollar bill on the bar before she could reach into her purse to pay. "That's on me. Now please tell me your name." He leaned in, too close for Kellie, and she backed away. He reeked of cheap cologne.

"K.C.," she said, with a glance to Will.

"I don't remember any gorgeous girls named Casey in high school." He leaned an arm on the bar and gave her the once-over, sending slimy chills down her back.

"Hmm, I don't really remember you, either." She picked up her glass.

"What do you do, Casey?" Scott asked, his rat eyes boring into her.

"I work at Channel 8," she said, staring at Will and avoiding eye contact with Scott.

"Hey, babe." Joe's voice behind her made her smile. Leave it to the movie director to know when to enter a scene.

She turned and laid a hand on Joe's shoulder. "Joey, do you know these men?"

She took a slight step back so she could watch.

"I sure do. Scott Hunter and Will…something," he said with a dismissive wave of his hand.

"Wait," Scott said, looking from Kellie to Joe and back to Kellie. "You two are…*together?*" He used his finger to point from one to the other.

"She's with me," Joe said. "Who's here with you, this guy?" Then he clapped Scott on the shoulder, hard enough for Scott to wince. Kellie grinned and walked away with Joe's arm around her waist.

"Thank you," she whispered as they walked back to their table.

"You were brilliant," he whispered back as they rejoined Suzanne and two other couples, all of whom were star struck to be sitting with the famous Joe Traversa.

*

After dinner and dancing, but before it was time to call it a night, Tiffany pushed Cherry Weiss-Patel's chair up to a microphone at the DJ station. The DJ lowered the mike to her level and tapped it a few times to get everyone's attention.

"Hey, everyone. Just wanted to say a few words. First, thanks to all of you for coming to this reunion!" She waited for the smattering of applause to end. "Our class never had a fifth, or a tenth, a fifteenth, or a twentieth reunion, but I wasn't about to let our twenty-fifth pass without a chance to reunite. Now, as much as I'd like to do a cheer for you all, I think it might be better if you just imagine me doing one." She glanced around at the kind faces smiling at her.

"As I said, I want to thank all of you for coming tonight. Some of you didn't have to travel very far; I know there are some who still live in West Alton and have witnessed the many changes in our little town over the past twenty-five years. We now have three supermarkets, four gas stations, and, of course, a drive-through coffee shop."

She caught Joe's eye, and he gave her a slight nod. She continued. "The person who probably traveled the farthest to come here is also the person who might be the best known. We all knew Joey Traversa in school. Really, who had more friends than Joe? And now we can boast that we knew him when. Before he packed up and headed west, before he started directing movies, and before he was an Oscar-winning director. Everybody, Joe Traversa."

Joe stood to loud applause and a whistle from Suzanne. He buttoned his suit jacket and pushed his blond hair from his tanned forehead, then walked to the microphone. Bending at the waist to kiss and hug Cherry, he then raised the microphone to a comfortable height and began speaking.

"Thank you. I'm really glad to be back among friends, here in Rhode Island. You know, I left here right after graduation, and if I had waited, perhaps I would have chickened out." He looked around the room and out of the corner of his eye, he saw Scott Hunter back at the bar, with his friend Will and another guy. That must be Robbie, Joe thought. He quelled the tremors in his gut and continued.

"High school presents us with challenges. Every day. Who likes us, who doesn't. Who cares? We all cared back then. It was important for me to be liked, a lot more important than it is now. You all knew I was gay then. Right? Oh no, am I shocking you?" Everyone in the room laughed with him. Joe saw Scott swivel around on his barstool to face him.

"It was hard to be gay! Even if the eighties afforded some fabulous fashion opportunities. It was still hard. I know I wasn't the only one." He saw a few people crane their necks to look around the room. His voice grew more serious. "It wasn't a choice. It's just who I am. But I paid a price for not hiding it, because there were people who harassed, intimidated, and threatened me." At this point, he focused on Scott Hunter at the bar. "The night before I starred as Pippin in our senior play, I was assaulted by a group of three men who were homophobic and violent." At the sound of gasps from the attendees, he paused. "Fortunately, fate or God intervened, I'm still not sure which, but I was spared some real bodily injury. All because I was, and am, a gay man. For no other reason."

Joe lifted his face and stood straight, the way his father had taught him. "Now, I'm famous. I'm accomplished, well-respected in my field. And yes, I'm paid well for the work I do. But more importantly, I'm not afraid. I'm not ashamed. And I'm even willing to buy those men a beer." He smiled at Scott, who quickly turned his back.

Joe grinned, his dazzlingly white teeth making him look more like a movie star than a director. Then he turned his attention to Suzanne and Kellie. "I'm here with my old - but not *old* - friend, Suzanne Fitch, and I couldn't have asked for a truer friend over the years. And with Cherry's permission, I'd like to introduce one more person to you tonight. I'm proud to call this woman my friend. Come on," he said with a tilt of his head to Kellie, who stood up and joined him at the microphone.

"Some of you think she's my date. Come on, it's me," he said, spreading his palms out while everyone chuckled. "She'll introduce herself." He kissed Kellie on the cheek and walked back to his table.

Kellie stood in front of the microphone. She looked at Cherry, who put both thumbs up right in front of her chest. She thought she would be more nervous, but calm settled inside her.

"I don't know if any of you will remember me. I look different than I did in high school." She took a deep breath and let it out slowly. Dear God, help me do this right, she prayed silently.

"My name is Kellie Blunt, although now I'm known as Kellie Campbell." She waited for it to sink in but wouldn't look at anyone, choosing instead, as Joe had suggested, to focus on a far corner of the room. She stared down a beige curtain. "In some ways, I was a very different person twenty-five years ago. I suppose we can all say that." She dared to glance at her best friend, and saw her face, her beautiful face, encouraging her to go on. And Joe, right next to her.

Kellie licked her dry lips and continued. "I wasn't like a lot of you. I lived in a trailer with my mom and my brother. I never knew my father." She added, "I knew who he was; my mother told me all about him, but I never met him."

Joe walked over with a glass of water and she took a sip. "We were poor," she said with a laugh. "Really poor. One week we ate ramen noodles every night of the week, but my mother would have us pretend we were Asian royalty because we got to eat ramen noodles." She raised her eyes briefly, as if her mother was in the ceiling smiling down on her. "My mom could sew, and she made me some pretty hideous clothes to wear to school. Then she decided to do some tie-dyeing, because she'd worn tie-dyed clothes when I was born. And as much as I wanted to tell her that no one was wearing tie-dye in 1988, I couldn't. Because everything she did, everything was for her children." Kellie felt the pressure behind her eyes as tears built up, but she pressed on.

"I was the weird kid, I know. I had a big nose. I had bad teeth because there was no money for braces. And I know you're wondering about this face, thinking I had work done. Yes, I have had work done." She looked up and saw a couple of smug smiles on the faces of women she didn't recognize. "I was a victim of domestic violence," she said directly to those women, whose smiles froze on their tight faces. Then she smiled. "But I'm okay now. He's gone."

Kellie felt she had said enough; she needed to wrap it up. "I wish I'd had the chance to know some of you in high school. I was shy, and because of that, I missed out on a lot, on social activities and dances and friendships. I hope that your children won't ignore the shy kid in school. Sometimes they're just hoping someone will talk to them." She was done. Maybe this was a bad idea. No one was clapping; they just stared at her. But as she stepped away from the microphone, her classmates, who had never bothered with ugly Kellie Blunt, stood up and surrounded her, offering a hand, a hug, a kind word.

Just then there was a commotion in the bar. "Holy shit! Scottso! You're on television!" The group moved *en masse*, like a herd, toward the bar in the back of the room, where the eleven o'clock news had just come on. "Turn it up!" Will shouted to the bartender. Everyone was quiet as the face of Jeff Braun appeared on the screen.

"In the last of our series on disability pensions, we have Scott Hunter, a lifelong resident of West Alton who served on the town's fire department until ten years ago, when after an unwitnessed fall in the station, he left the department with a permanent back injury. Mr. Hunter collects approximately forty thousand dollars a year, tax free, for his alleged disability. Here's some of the footage we shot of Mr. Hunter and his back injury."

Everyone in attendance then watched film of Scott jumping on his motorcycle, with Molly behind him. One hand wrapped around his waist while the other used her cell phone to record the journey. Next up was Scott running into the ocean, jumping the waves, running back out and flopping on the blanket next to Molly. There was even footage of Scott hoisting Molly above his head, laughing and squeezing her bottom.

"Son of a bitch," Scott muttered, loud enough for some to hear.

The sound of Will laughing was the only noise. The attendees murmured to each other, and Kellie, flanked by Suzanne and Joe, walked up to the bar as Scott turned around. She held her coat over her arm. With one look back, she caught Scott's eye. Kellie nodded to him, then turned and walked out the door with her friends.

THE END

About the Author

Martha Reynolds ended an accomplished career as a fraud investigator in 2011 and began pursuing a lifelong dream of writing. She is the author and publisher of five novels, including the award-winning *Chocolate for Breakfast* (book one in The Chocolate Series), *Chocolate Fondue*, *Bittersweet Chocolate*, and the Amazon bestseller *Bits of Broken Glass*.

Her very short poem was featured in Tell Me More's Twitter Poetry Challenge, and she has contributed essays and reflections to *Magnificat* magazine.

She and her husband live in Rhode Island, never far from the ocean.

Connect with Martha:

Facebook:
http://www.facebook.com/MarthaReynoldsWriter

Twitter: @TheOtherMartha1

Blog: http://MarthaReynoldsWrites.com